ELISABETH DAHL

Amulet Books ★ New York

Library of Congress Cataloging-in-Publication Data
Dahl, Elisabeth, 1969–
Genie wishes / by Elisabeth Dahl.
pages cm
Summary: Follows fifth-grader Genie Kunkle through a tumultuous year at Hopkins Country Day School, as a new girl tries to take Genie's place as Sarah's best friend, and Genie learns that expressing her opinion in public can be scary when she is elected class blogger.
ISBN 978-1-4197-0526-7 (alk. paper)
[1. Schools—Fiction. 2. Best friends—Fiction. 3. Friendship—Fiction.
4. Blogs—Fiction. 5. Baltimore (Md.)—Fiction.] I. Title.
PZ7.D15116Ge 2013
[Fic]—dc23
2012033161

Text and illustrations copyright © 2013 Elisabeth Dahl
Book design by Sara Corbett

Printed and bound in USA
10 9 8 7 6 5 4 3 2

Amulet Books are available at special discounts when purchased in quantity for premiums and promotions as well as fundraising or educational use. Special editions can also be created to specification. For details, contact specialsales@abramsbooks.com or the address below.

THE ART OF BOOKS SINCE 1949
115 West 18th Street
New York, NY 10011
www.abramsbooks.com

FOR
Jackson

CHAPTER 1

Class List

O n the last day of summer break, as I darted into the kitchen for another cherry Twin Pop, I spotted the yellow envelope from school on the counter. I grabbed the Twin Pop and the envelope and ran back outside to Sarah, who was jumping back and forth over the spouting-whale sprinkler. I broke the Twin Pop in two with a thwack and handed her half, then ripped into the envelope and pulled out the new class list.

Sarah stood behind me, her chin resting on my shoulder. "We're in the same homeroom!" she squealed.

"Look," I said, pointing to a name I'd never seen before. "Blair Annabelle Lea." We hadn't had a new classmate since

1

second grade. Her name sounded like something out of *Gone with the Wind*, a movie I'd just watched with my grandmother.

"Oh my gosh, I totally forgot to tell you she was coming to HCD! She went to my camp," Sarah said. "She's the one who made me this bracelet." She pointed to the braided leather bracelet on her wrist, the thickest of the friendship bracelets she'd returned from camp with a couple of weeks earlier. "She's so cool. I told her all about you."

A water droplet fell from my hair to the paper, landing on Blair's name, where it wiggled and shimmered in the sunlight.

The next morning, fifteen fifth graders—exactly half the class—started piling into each of the two fifth-grade classrooms, which sat like anchors at the end of a long hallway. The fifth-grade classrooms were big, with windows facing two directions and desks with padded seats.

Sarah and I met in the hallway by our new lockers, then walked together into Mr. Sayler's room. "Blair's coming late," Sarah said. "They just moved here from DC. It's totally *complicated*."

Complicated? That didn't sound like a Sarah word.

During third period we lined up by class on the auditorium's long wooden benches for the first-day assembly. Sarah and I sat next to each other, both wearing white running shoes with red details. Her shoelaces were a brighter white than mine, as always. Her mother had secret laundry tricks.

Once all the classes were seated, Mr. Frazier, the music teacher, launched into "We're All Together Again" on the piano. As fifth graders—the seniors of the lower school—we knew to sing out very loudly during this song, just a notch below what Mr. Frazier would call *obnoxious*. It was what fifth graders always did on the first day of school.

"Is the fifth grade here?" Mr. Frazier sang.

"We're here! We're here!"

"Is the fifth grade here?"

"WE'RE HERE! WE'RE HERE!"

Mr. Graham, the Hopkins Country Day head-master, walked onto the stage, and we quieted down. "Welcome, everyone, to another great year at HCD," he said.

Just then, a single pair of heels clicked across the back of the auditorium's wooden floor. We all turned around to see a girl standing at the top of the center aisle. She had long white-blond hair, shoes with little heels, and a hot-pink tote bag that said "BOYZZZZ!"

"That's Blair!" Sarah whispered loudly.

At lunch, Blair sat with Sarah, Rebecca, and me. Rebecca's tray had two fish sandwiches, bean soup, a banana, two milks, and a chocolate chip cookie. Blair's had an orange and a packet of saltines. Sarah's and mine were somewhere in the middle.

"Are you ten or eleven?" Rebecca asked Blair.

"Eleven," Blair said, jiggling her knee under the table. "I turned eleven at camp this summer. Oh my

God, Sare, I forgot to tell you. Ethan totally texted me."

"Oh my God!" Sarah said.

"You have a phone?" Rebecca asked.

"Of course," Blair said.

"My parents say it's unnecessary," Rebecca said.

"Sare, you have one, right?" Blair asked.

"I wish."

"Jennie?"

"It's Genie," I said. "No, I don't." Had Sarah really told her about me? She didn't even know my name.

The more Blair jiggled her leg, the more the milk in my carton swished around stormily.

"We have e-mail," Rebecca said.

"E-mail's, like, so three years ago," Blair said.

"I'm begging my mom to give me her old iPhone," Sarah said. "Maybe for Christmas."

"If you do get a phone, you-know-who is going to text you," said Blair.

"Wes?" Sarah asked.

"Duh!"

"No way."

"You have to check the Seawind Web site. Some-one posted a photo of you at the talent show and Wes wrote 'prettiest camper' in the comments."

"He did not!" Sarah squealed.

It didn't seem like the time to mention that I'd learned to do a flip off the diving board this summer. Rebecca wasn't volunteering any more information either.

The school assigned lockers alphabetically, and Blair's was next to mine. Mr. Sayler, our homeroom teacher, had printed out each of our names in this fancy cursive font and taped them just above the locker vents. At the end of the first day, as we packed up our bags in the hallway, Blair looked at the name label on my locker. "Genie Haddock Kunkle," she said. "Isn't *haddock* the name of a fish? Are your parents, like, fishermen or something?"

"It was my mother's last name."

"Oh," she said.

"My dad's an artist. He teaches art classes at MAC. Maryland Art College."

"Oh," she said.

I'd never liked Haddock Kunkle much myself. It sounded like the name of some weird instrument you'd only see in music class. (As in, "Genie, it's your turn to play the haddock kunkle now!") But I'd never thought about the fish part until this moment, as I watched Blair saunter off down the hall in her pointy little heels.

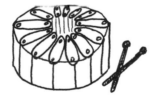

the haddock kunkle

CHAPTER 2

Election

On the second day of school, Mr. Sayler announced that HCD was starting a new program: class blogs on the school Web site. He passed around a sign-up sheet and asked students to write down their names if they were interested in serving as the fifth grade's class blogger.

Rebecca raised her skinny arm as high as it would go, and Mr. Sayler called on her. "I don't really get it," she said, scrunching up her face.

"Have you guys read blogs before?" Mr. Sayler asked. "The ones some teachers have on the HCD Web site, for instance? Raise your hand if you've ever read a blog." Most people raised their hands.

The only blog I'd ever read was my grandmother's. She was the school librarian, so she posted Dewey decimal quizzes, pictures of new books they'd gotten in the library, authors' photos—stuff like that.

"But what would the blogger actually *do*?" Rebecca asked.

"Once every week or so, the class blogger would write a post about something that the class has been doing or saying or thinking about. The theme for all the classes' blogs this year is Wishes, Hopes, and Dreams."

A few people groaned.

"What?" Mr. Sayler said. He leaned against his desk, knocking over his jar of pens and pencils by mistake. One time I'd heard my grandmother tell my dad that Mr. Sayler was a "hippy man." At first I thought she meant he was a hippie, and I wasn't sure why, because he didn't have long hair, and he seemed to dress like all the other teachers. Later I realized that she meant "hippy," as in having big hips. For a man.

"Wishes, Hopes, and Dreams," Drew said, making every word sound puffed up and sugary, like meringue. "Sounds boring."

"Well, *you* don't have to run for class blogger, then," Mr. Sayler said, shoving pens and pencils back into the jar. "Not every blog post has to address the theme directly. It's more like a touchstone for the blogs, something to keep in mind as the year goes on. The teachers will review the list of interested candidates, then pick two people—one boy and one girl—to run. You guys will get to vote tomorrow, right before lunch."

Our class had voted about little things before, like whether to stay inside or go outside for recess, but we'd never had an election for something this major. When the paper came across my desk, I looked at it for a second, then passed it to the next person.

A class blogger probably needed to be loud and outgoing, I figured—a kind of town crier, like the ones we'd learned about in history class, the person whose job it was to stand in the middle of a town shouting out information. Rebecca might be a good one. Or maybe our newest classmate, Blair. But I wasn't right for the job.

꘎◗)(◖꘎

When we were waiting for carpool that day, Sarah asked if I had put my name on the class blogger list.

"No," I said.

"Why not? You're an awesome writer!"

"Did you sign up?"

"You know I can barely spell," she said.

"That doesn't matter," I said.

"Yes, it does. But *you* should do it! Teachers always ask you to read aloud from stuff you write!" She turned sideways until our backpacks banged into each other. She kept swiveling and banging, smiling at me. "Come on, do it!"

Was she right?

At dinner, I told everyone in the house—my dad, my grandmother, and my fourteen-year-old brother, Ian—about the blogger election. Dad and Gran said I should go for it. Ian didn't say anything.

My grandfather would have encouraged me to run for class blogger too, if he had still been alive. Last spring we'd come home from the grocery store and found him lying in his rock garden. A heart attack, the doctor had said. Sometimes, I still saw Granddad working out there among the plants, wearing his mustard-yellow gardening gloves.

Dad, Ian, and I had moved into my grandparents' house when I was four years old, just after my mother died in a car accident. She probably would have encouraged me to run for class blogger too, but it was harder to be sure about her. I didn't really remember her like I remembered Granddad.

Gran and I had bedrooms on the second floor, and Dad and Ian on the third floor. It was a good thing my parents hadn't had any more kids, because there weren't any other bedrooms.

Because Gran was the school librarian, we paid half as much tuition, Dad said. Otherwise, we never could have afforded HCD. Ian went to HCD through fifth grade but then switched to Guilford Middle, our neighborhood school, which Dad said was a better fit for him.

That night, when I was under the covers and reading, my grandmother stopped by my room. Bobby pins held her hair in flat curls against her head, the way they did every night. When she took the bobby pins out the next morning, soft waves would frame her face. She still wore her hair the way it was when she met my grandfather.

"I really do hope you toss your name into the hat," she said, fidgeting with a bobby pin.

"I don't think I'm going to."

"Why not?"

"Shouldn't the class blogger be—I don't know—more of a loudmouth? Someone who likes the spotlight?"

"Not at all! The class blogger will be speaking on behalf of the whole grade, so she—or he—would have to be a good listener as well as a good writer. You'd be a natural. If I were you, I'd get myself on the list."

Were Sarah and Gran right? Should I really run for class blogger?

That night, I dreamed I was flying over Baltimore, but I wasn't high above everything, brushing up against the clouds. Instead, I was flying low, close enough to touch the blue-gray rooftops and the topmost leaves of the trees. I glided over our neighborhood's row houses, then over the triangular park where I used to play catch with my grandfather. I'd never dreamed about flying before.

⚭)(⚭

The next morning, I asked Mr. Sayler if it was too late to add my name to the list of potential class bloggers.

"You're just in time," he said, smiling and handing me the sheet. There had to have been twenty names on it.

During recess, Mr. Sayler and the other fifth-grade teacher, Ms. Durst, narrowed the list down to two candidates. One was Hassan, a boy from my homeroom who had been planning to be a surgeon since he was two years old and hated to lose at anything, even some random race in PE. The other was me. Me!

Recently, Gran had taught me the word *gamboling*, which means "leaping playfully"—racing and jumping around. That's what my heart was doing after I heard my name.

Before lunch, the whole fifth grade packed into Mr. Sayler's room. We each wrote down the name of one candidate and put our ballots into a shoe box. Then Mr. Sayler counted out the papers one by one while Ms. Durst sat next to him on the desk. In the end, Hassan lost by just two votes. I couldn't help looking at him, at the jaw muscles clenching on the side of his face. Sarah gave me a high five.

"All right!" Mr. Sayler said. "Well, congratulations, Genie. Remind me to give you the class-blogger instruction sheet before you leave today. You can get started on blogging whenever you're ready, even tonight. And the rest of you: remember to read the blog posts and add comments whenever you have something to say!"

My heart was still gamboling around, but my head saw flashing red lights. Now that I'd been elected, I wasn't so sure that running for class blogger had been a good idea. I'd even hesitated about voting for myself when the time came. What would I blog about?

⁓◌) (◌⁓

"You guys?" Rebecca said, spooning up her beef barley soup at lunch. "You know what my mom told me this morning? The parents' association made the cafeteria people take Junk Food Lunch off the menu." Rebecca's mom was our class parent this year, as she almost always was, so she knew these things.

Jack, who was sitting at the next table over, whipped his head around. "Holy guacamole!" he said. "Frittata maraca, hakuna matata! What did you say?"

"The parents' association got rid of Junk Food Lunch."

"No way!" he said.

"Junk Food Lunch is really good!" Rebecca told Blair. "They give you pizza and french fries and cake and ice cream and burgers and cookies and practically everything."

Blair shrugged her shoulders.

Jack told everyone at the other tables. Soon the whole fifth grade knew that Junk Food Lunch was a thing of the past.

"Oh no!" Anna Miles said. "Junk Food Lunch is my favorite thing about school! My dads *never* let me have junk food at home!"

At HCD, you couldn't bring your own food to lunch. Unless you had serious allergies, you had to eat what the cafeteria provided, so people were extra-invested in what the cafeteria served.

"Genie," Sarah said, "you've got to do a blog entry about it."

"Awesome idea!" Jack said.

"Okay," I said. "I will." Phew—at least I had *one* thing to write about.

"If you convince them to bring Junk Food Lunch back, I'll be *soooo* happy," Rebecca said, wrapping a skinny arm around my shoulders. "I'll give you three more hamster erasers!" Hamster erasers fell off your pencil all the time, they didn't erase very well, and their whiskers snapped off easily, but they were really cute.

"Blogs are so, like, three years ago," Blair said, rolling her eyes.

Was there such a thing as a transitive property of friendship, like the transitive properties we learned about in math class? You know, where if A is equal to B, and B is equal to C, then A is equal to C? Or if A is greater than B, and B is greater than C, then A is greater than C? Blair (A) was friends with Sarah (B), and Sarah (B) was friends with me (C). But that didn't make C and A friends automatically, did it?

Sarah and I had been best friends for what felt like forever, and we had made a lot of plans about what we'd do when we grew up. We'd be roommates and have an apartment downtown on the harbor and walk to our jobs as dolphin trainers at the National Aquarium. Then we'd have a double wedding in which we'd marry best friends, and then we'd buy houses on the same block. That was as far as we'd gotten.

During our last-period study hall, Mr. Sayler invited me up to his desk to go over the class-blogger instruction sheet.

"It's all fairly straightforward," Mr. Sayler said. "But if you need help, you can shoot me an e-mail. You feel good about this?"

"I guess so," I said.

"You'll be great," he said. "No worries."

During carpool that day, Sarah and I talked about the election. I still couldn't believe I'd beaten Hassan. Sarah said she wasn't surprised at all. She thought that some people didn't like Hassan because he could be a know-it-all.

We decided I should have a blogger name. A pen name. A lot of writers used them, Sarah said. So she got out her purple pen that smelled like grape, and we brainstormed. We talked about the blog theme of Wishes, Hopes, and Dreams and how it related to my name. It took only about one minute to think of *Genie Wishes*.

Genie Wishes!

"Drew will hate it!" Sarah said, laughing. "It's perfect!" Drew was Sarah's cousin, and she liked to torture him.

Genie Wishes was not Genie Haddock Kunkle. The name didn't have anything to do with weird musical instruments or fish. It sounded breezy with possibility, like a wide-open window with gauzy drapes.

At dinner, I told everyone about winning the blogger election. Dad and Gran were happy for me. But Ian? Other than laughing at the name Genie Wishes, which I knew he would, Ian barely looked up from his spaghetti.

After I finished my homework that night, I typed

my first blog entry on Dad's computer, following the instructions Mr. Sayler had given me. I didn't know whether I would be a good blogger, but at least I had a cool blogger name and, more important, a first topic.

Junk Food Lunch?

Word got out today that the parents' association decided to do away with Junk Food Lunch. The fifth grade is really sad! Junk Food Lunch was one of the best things at HCD!

Wish #1: That Junk Food Lunch would come back!

Signed,
Genie Wishes
Fifth-Grade Class Blogger

I decided to send the draft to Mr. Sayler, to ask whether the post was okay in general and whether it would be all right to include a wish with every blog post.

He wrote back almost immediately.

It looks great, Genie! I love the idea of including one wish per blog post.

No need to clear the posts with me first, though. The IT guys will be scanning them all before they are posted to the site, just to ensure that the content is appropriate, but I don't think we need to worry about that with you!

Have a good night.

Mr. Sayler

P.S. Some of us teachers also wouldn't mind if Junk Food Lunch came back.

I read the blog post one more time, then uploaded it. I waited fifteen minutes at the computer for someone to read it and comment, but nothing happened, so I took a shower and got into bed to read.

CHAPTER 3

Comments

First thing the next morning, I checked Dad's computer. Three people had commented on my blog post! Three! My heart skipped not one but two beats.

....

JACK   Even if we just had pizza once in a while, that would be great. You wouldn't even have to call it Junk Food Lunch.

....

ANNA MILES   Totally. Go Genie Wishes!

....

MACY   My mother says Junk Food Lunch teaches you bad habits. I hate to tell you guys, but it's probably good that they ended it.

While I was sitting at the computer thinking about how strict Macy's mother was, another comment appeared!

....

REBECCA   OMG! OMG! OMG! Pleazzzzzze! I am the Number One Junk Food Lunch Lover!

This cracked me up. Rebecca was so skinny, hugging her felt like hugging a wire hanger. As Gran would say, Where did she *put* all that food? People would be more likely to look at me and guess that *I* was the Number One Junk Food Lunch Lover.

It was still early September, but today already felt like autumn, so I went to my dresser and pulled out a new corduroy skirt that Gran and I had found on a clearance rack two months earlier. I took off my pajama bottoms and changed my underwear, then slid the skirt up past my knees. The skirt had fit in the dressing room in July, but I'd eaten a lot of Twin Pops since then. Would it still zip up at the waist?

I'd worried about things fitting ever since two Christmases before, when Gran had given me these awesome knee-high zip-up boots with fur around the top. I hadn't been able to zip the boots up all the way, no matter how much I'd tugged, and I'd started to cry. Then Dad and I had gone into my bedroom and had a talk about how Dad thought I looked just right— not too thin, not too heavy. I'd said that *Tween Life* models are always really skinny, and he'd said that ideas about what is beautiful change over time—that lots of artists in history preferred to draw people who looked like me, people who were more than just sticks.

But the corduroy skirt still fit! I ran my hands along its soft ribbing as I looked in my closet in search of a shirt.

∞◗)(◖∞

While we waited for Mr. Sayler to start our day's first class—History—I talked to Sarah at her desk, which was next to mine and directly in front of Blair's. Blair had her phone nestled in her lap and was tapping something into it—a major no-no during school hours.

Sarah opened her history book and pointed to a name from the chapter we'd read for homework. "How do you pronounce this guy's name?"

"I think it's *Fuh-dip-uh-dees*," I said.

"Phidippides," Sarah repeated. "I love that name."

"I know. It's so funny," I said.

"I wonder if the whole time he was running between Athens and Sparta, he was thinking *Phi-DIP-pi-des, Phi-DIP-pi-des*," Sarah said.

Sarah and I both jumped up and started pretending we were running that way, saying one syllable per step. We started giggling uncontrollably. Soon I was laughing so hard, I felt as if my legs wouldn't hold me up.

"Ewww!" Blair said suddenly, pointing at my legs. "Why don't you shave them?"

I looked down. My legs looked like they always did, tapering and pale and covered with light brown hair. My left knee had a faint scar shaped like a boomerang, from kneeling on a piece of glass when I was five or six years old.

"I've been shaving my legs since I was seven!" Blair said.

"Blair . . . ," Sarah said.

"Okay, class, sorry for the delay," Mr. Sayler said, standing up behind his desk.

I'd never even realized you were *supposed* to shave your legs. I mean, I knew a lot of women did, but I'd never thought about *me* shaving *my* legs.

Back in my desk chair, I studied the girls in my homeroom. Four out of eight had smooth, smooth legs. Blair was one of them, of course. Sarah, I was surprised to see, was too. Had she always shaved her legs?

CHAPTER 4

Slumber Party

my grandmother would have said that Blair's comment about my legs took the wind out of my sails. And she would have been right. A whole week had passed, but I was still thinking about it.

I was also starting to wonder what my next blog post should be. I couldn't think of anything important that had happened in school in the last week. We'd been getting to know our new teachers, reviewing last year's math—stuff like that. Fifth grade had barely even started.

Then I remembered that Sarah was having a party. All the girls in the class were invited, and it involved wishes, hopes, and dreams—sort of.

I set to work on a new blog post.

Sleepover!

I'm not sure what the fifth-grade boys are doing this Saturday night, but I know what all the girls are doing: having a sleepover at Sarah's house! First we have to help out at the parents' cocktail party downstairs. Then we get to have our own party! It's going to be so fun!

Wish #2: That we don't run out of popcorn before we run out of movies.

I sent the post to Mr. Sayler, to make sure it was okay. Here's what he wrote back:

> It looks good, Genie! But again, there's no need to clear posts with me. As I said the other day, the IT folks will sign off on every post before it goes onto the site.
>
> This is your space to do with what you will. Sometimes you'll be speaking *on behalf of* the class, and at other times you'll be speaking *to* the class. Often you'll be doing both!

You interpret the topic as you wish to interpret it, and remember, put as much of your own personality—your unique voice—into the blog posts as you like.

I uploaded the blog post. Pretty soon, I had comments again!

....

SARAH   Don't forget your sleeping bags, everybody!

....

JACK   Okay! Mine has rainbows and ponies on it.

....

BLAIR   OMG you know you are so not invited!!!!

....

REBECCA   No boys allowed!

....

JACK   Waaaahhh. Sob. I WISH I was coming!

"A cocktail party and a slumber party in one night?" Gran said to me later. "They're biting off more than they can chew." I knew she was wrong, though. Mrs. White—Sarah's mom—loved having parties, even two at a time.

On Saturday afternoon, I washed my hair with the apple-smelling shampoo I loved, then reached into the closet for a blue razor, the kind Gran used. I figured I should at least *try* shaving my legs. If I didn't like it, I could always stop.

I pulled the razor up the center of my left leg from the ankle to the knee, right over the boomerang scar. When I touched the skin the razor had passed over, it felt whispery smooth. I kept going, strip by strip, just the way I did when I helped my dad mow the lawn.

I stepped out of the shower, dried off with a towel, and examined my new legs. Though they might feel whispery smooth, my new legs didn't actually look very different from my old legs.

All the girls arrived at Sarah's at six thirty. We

dropped off our stuff in Sarah's room. Then we went back to the front hall, and Mrs. White showed us how to lay out the name tags, how to take people's coats, and how to show guests to the study, where the party would be. I loved the Whites' house. It always smelled really clean—like a nice store.

While we were working on the name tags, Sophie, a girl in the other homeroom, asked me if it was hard to write a blog, and I said yes, a little, and that I was still figuring it out. I didn't know Sophie that well because we'd never been in the same homeroom, but we were always in English together, and she was nice. She had curly hair that was really black and glossy, and when she pulled it down straight, you couldn't believe how long it was.

"Where's Nora?" asked Bethany. Nora was Sarah's little sister.

"Spending the night at a friend's," said Sarah.

"Where's Blair?" asked Bethany.

"Coming late," Sarah said. "She had to go to some other party with her parents first."

I went to use one of the Whites' downstairs bathrooms before the parents started arriving. To get to the bathroom, I passed through the Whites' gigantic kitchen, where five or six grown-ups wearing all-black uniforms were arranging food on platters. There were three whole trays just for shrimp! Granddad would have been so happy. He always used to ask Gran to make shrimp on his birthday.

The bathroom walls had this satiny pink-and-green-striped wallpaper and framed pictures from books like *Babar.* The overhead light was frosty and soft, and there was an oval bar of soap that made your hands smell like grapefruit.

After I used the bathroom and washed my hands, I lingered, taking a deep breath. Was it weird that one of my favorite rooms anywhere was a bathroom?

∞◗) (◖∞

Pretty soon the front hall was filling up with grown-ups. We all worked as a team. I was on coatroom duty, and there were a lot of coats coming in. Even though it was only late September, it was chilly, the kind of night where you wore the wintry clothes you'd bought in August just because you wanted to wear them, even if it wasn't really cold enough yet. Some of the coats were heavy, with bright, silky linings. Rebecca's mom's gloves were the softest things I had ever felt. I'd once read in *Tween Life* about "buttery" leather, but I hadn't understood what that meant until now.

We were back in what the Whites called the media room watching our first movie when Blair came in, rolling a suitcase behind her like a flight attendant. Her white-blond hair had been curled into fat spirals, and she wore a minidress the color of a traffic cone. Rebecca paused the movie.

"How was the party?" Sarah asked.

"Oh, y'know," Blair said. "They're all the same."

"They who?" Bethany asked.

"The parties."

"What parties?" Bethany asked.

"For my dad's new job. We have to go to a lot of parties."

"What's his job?" Bethany asked.

"President of Kirkland University."

"Cool," Bethany said. "Where was the party tonight?"

"The governor's mansion."

"Oh my God! Did you meet her?"

"Yeah," Blair said. "We bonded." She took a can of diet soda off the side table and squeezed between Sarah and Rebecca on the sofa.

Dad stopped by the media room a few minutes later, wearing his brown tweed sportcoat, white button-down shirt, and corduroys: the same clothes he wore if he had to go to church for some reason. Normally, even on days he was teaching, he wore T-shirts and jeans. I gave him a hug, and he said hi to everyone. After he left, Bethany said he was really cute. I wasn't sure about that. He was tall and had lots of dark hair and big straight teeth. He also had a potbelly and really knobby knees and did not always brush his teeth before bed.

Gran could have come to the party, I guess, since she was sort of like my other parent, but she didn't. Since she was the librarian, she got invited to all the faculty parties, and between that and church activities I think she had enough socializing. She was probably sitting at home in her plaid flannel nightgown, eating popcorn and watching *Brit Wit* on PBS. She loved *Brit Wit*.

~◌)) (◌~

We finished watching our first movie: *Rink-and-Roll*. It was about an ice skater who broke her leg and couldn't skate anymore but then joined a rock band and was happy again. Before the next movie started, Sarah and I peeked into the study.

"Those are Blair's parents," Sarah whispered, pointing to the man in the tuxedo and the woman in the gold sequined dress standing by the bar. Both were tilting their heads back and laughing at something the bartender was saying.

Dad was seated on the other side of the room in a big leather chair, talking to a few parents. He was drinking a beer, and his face was kind of flushed. He looked toward us, excused himself, and walked over.

"How are you girls holding up?"

"We're having a great time," I said. Sarah nodded.

"Are you gonna be all right to spend the night?" he asked me.

"Yep."

"Okay. Don't stay up too late. Gran will be here at nine o'clock sharp."

"Good night, Mr. Kunkle," Sarah said. I kissed Dad on the cheek, and we headed back to the media room.

"Bethany's right, your dad is *so* adorable," Sarah said. "Why doesn't he have a girlfriend?"

"I don't know," I said. "I totally want him to go on Soulmates.com."

"He should!" Sarah said, clapping her hands.

Then Blair ran over, grabbed Sarah by the elbow, and whisked her off somewhere.

∽◌) (◌∾

Everyone got tired during the second movie, not long after we finished our eighth batch of microwave popcorn and used the last of the temporary tattoos.

With backpacks, duffel bags, and sleeping bags scattered all over the rug, it was hard to walk around Sarah's room. Rebecca, Sarah, and I put on T-shirts and sleep shorts. Blair put on a red, white, and blue tank top that said "All-American" and matching shorts that spelled "Trouble" across her butt.

"Oh my God," Blair announced, pointing to me. "Genie started shaving her legs!"

"It's no big deal," I said, blushing.

I tucked my smooth legs into the sleeping bag and closed my eyes. It was two o'clock now, later than I'd ever stayed up. My tongue felt dry and my eyes stung.

I heard Blair say that at her old school the boys

used to snap the back straps of girls' bras all the time. She asked if that ever happened at HCD, and a few people with older sisters said yes but it hadn't happened in our class yet.

Bra snapping? It sounded painful.

Then I heard Blair ask if anyone in the class had gotten her period yet, and everyone said no. She told a story about a fourth grader at her old school who'd gotten her period for the first time on a field trip. She'd had to borrow a pad from a teacher and put it on in the public restroom at the National Gallery of Art. Rebecca said that if that happened to her on a field trip, she'd die.

Bethany said she'd heard a story about a second grader at HCD getting her period, but she wasn't sure whether it was true.

Then Anna Miles said someone in her neighborhood had gotten pregnant from kissing her boyfriend. The squeal that followed—which I had to assume came out of Blair—was so piercing, I was sure the Whites would be alarmed, but they didn't come to check on us.

Next, I heard Sarah suggest that we vote on our favorite teachers, but Blair said no, instead we should vote on who was the cutest boy in our class, with separate votes for best hair, best smile, et cetera. No one asked for my vote. They thought I was asleep.

The last thing I remember, Blair was rooting around for her cell phone so she could text the contest results to the boys.

∽◐) (◑∼

I was dressed and ready to go when Gran picked me up for church the next morning. Unlike the chilly night before, the morning was kind of warm, so I wasn't wearing my coat. Gran looked alarmed by the dragon tattoo on my arm, but I knew the choir robe would hide it. Our youth choir was performing one song during the service.

Gran took me to church every week because she said it was important to have a good foundation. Dad didn't go, and neither did Ian. When Ian turned thirteen, Gran had given him a choice, and he'd chosen to stop. I didn't mind it at church. I had my friends that I hung out with, and I liked how the sound of the organ swelled through the pews and up to the ceiling. The sound was loud but deep and calming, not at all like the sounds that came out of Blair.

CHAPTER 5

Row Houses

One October day, Sarah and I were sitting under a tree during recess. Half the fifth graders were playing four-square, and the other half, kickball. Blair hopped on one foot in the four-square line, talking to Drew and Jack.

"We have to decide what to be for Halloween," Sarah said as she braided some grasses she'd pulled from the lawn. "My mom said she would drive us to the craft store after school today if we know what we want to get."

Because Gran worked just until noon and Sarah's house wasn't far from ours, Sarah's mom drove me home from school every day, along with Sarah, of course, and Sarah's little sister, Nora, a first grader. Mrs. White always had snacks and drinks for us. She liked us to tell her about what had happened at school, and as we'd talk she'd keep looking at us in the rear-view mirror. On sunny days she'd wear sunglasses with lenses that were practically as big as plates. Sometimes she'd push the glasses on top of her head, and you could see her long eyelashes. Mrs. White's hair was brown, like mine, but with light blond streaks.

The four-square ball rolled toward Sarah and me, so I picked it up and threw it back into the game.

"We could go as some food thing, like peanut butter and chocolate, or bread and butter," I said.

"Yeah," Sarah said. "That would be good." She didn't look up from her braiding, though. When Sarah liked something, it wasn't hard to tell. She didn't jump up and down or scream or anything, but she got a really big smile, and sometimes she clapped her hands.

"You know, a few years ago my parents went as Teletubbies to this big costume party," she said. "Their costumes are probably still in Mom's closet. They might be too big for us, but we could try them."

"My dad told me last week about a costume that

one of his art students created. It was a row house. He said it was cool. I was thinking we could hang cardboard row houses around our necks."

Sarah looked up from her grass braiding and smiled. "Yes! If we were each, like, three houses, then if we stood right next to each other, we'd be a whole row. Awesome! We can get the stuff at the store today."

"Actually, my dad probably already has everything we need," I said.

"Cool," Sarah said.

Then Blair ran over and tugged Sarah up by the elbow, saying Drew and Jack had something she *had* to see, and Sarah ran off.

On Saturday afternoon, Dad helped Sarah and me work on our costumes in the basement. First we laid heavy cloth tarps out on the cement floor. Then Dad spread out the paints and brushes he'd brought from his studio, along with sheets of cardboard he'd rescued from the recycling bin behind his building at MAC.

Sarah and I looked at the big, empty brown sheets, then at each other.

"Could you outline the houses for us?" Sarah asked my dad.

I knew my father wouldn't say yes to that, the same way my grandmother wouldn't just spell a word out loud when you asked her how. She always made you go to the huge dictionary in her bedroom.

"Maybe we should print out a picture of row houses off the Internet?" I suggested.

"Or, like, find a picture from a book about Baltimore?" Sarah said.

"Well, it depends on what type of row house you want to draw," Dad said. "You could just go out front and sketch our block, but if you really want the classic downtown Baltimore row house, with the white marble steps, you might want to draw from a picture. The row houses on our block are a later style."

"Let's draw the classic one," I said.

"Yeah," Sarah added.

We ran upstairs to the coffee table in the living

room, where Gran kept a picture book about Baltimore. We flipped through pages of monuments and churches, parks and dogwood trees, until we found some photos of row houses.

Dad looked over our shoulders. "Those would work," he said.

We sketched out some shapes on the cardboard. Sarah didn't like her sketch and said it would be better if I did both hers and mine, so that it looked like a single row of houses when we stood beside each other. I said okay.

"What color should we use for the brick? Just red?" Sarah asked.

"Maybe red with a little brown mixed in," I said. We worked on mixing, adding a little red here, a little brown there, until the color looked like real brick.

Except for the sound of Dad moving around upstairs, the house was quiet. Ian was out at a friend's, and Gran was at an organ concert at church.

"When's the last time you did a Genie Wishes post?" Sarah asked.

"A couple of weeks ago, I think. It's hard to know what to write about."

"The first two you did were great, though."

"Thanks."

Sarah dropped her voice to a whisper: "Did you get your dad on Soulmates.com yet?"

"Nope," I said, pulling a brushstroke of brownish red across the bottom of one house.

"This woman Caddie who gives me riding lessons is really pretty," Sarah said. "She looks like Sandra Bullock, and she lives on a farm. Maybe he could call her?"

"Dad doesn't like having friends set him up on dates. He says it makes him feel pressured to like the person."

"Oh," said Sarah.

We painted the windows white. For the front doors we used brown. And for the steps we used more white, with veins of gray snaking through, to make the steps look like real marble.

"I invited Blair to trick-or-treat with us," Sarah

said, "but she's going back to her old neighborhood in DC for Halloween this year."

I didn't say anything. Sarah and I had never trick-or-treated with anyone else, not even Rebecca, who we'd been friends with forever.

Dad came back downstairs and cut out the cardboard row houses using a special knife. Then Sarah and I poked holes at the top and ran string through the holes, so the cardboard would hang around our necks.

We laid the completed row houses back down on the floor and stood over them.

"Nice work," said Dad.

CHAPTER 6

Halloween

At ten thirty on Halloween morning, the whole fifth grade stood in the hallway by our lockers, waiting. In the distance, we could hear dozens of pairs of feet thwacking the linoleum, heading our way.

A firefighter appeared first. Behind her streamed other costumed kindergarteners in a single file. Bethany gave her little brother a high five when he walked by dressed as SpongeBob.

Some of my classmates complained that we didn't get to wear costumes. They were right! Why limit in-school Halloween to kindergarteners?

After school, I typed up a new blog post. I thought about asking Gran to read it first, but I remembered what Mr. Sayler had said about having confidence.

Halloween

Halloween at HCD is fun, and everyone loves the kindergarten parade, but some of us fifth graders think it would be even better if the whole school got to dress up!

Wish #3: That everyone at HCD, even the teachers, could dress up on Halloween!

....

(BETHANY) Totally!

....

(ANNA MILES) Yeah!

....

(JACK) That would be Super, man! (Get it???)

On Halloween night, Sarah and I got ready in her bedroom. Because the weather was colder than on most Halloweens, we wore black fleeces, turtlenecks, and jeans. Sarah let me borrow an extra pair of her UGGs, since all I'd brought were my Crocs. Sarah put her long blond hair up into a ponytail. I tried to do the same, but my brown hair was so short, half of it slid out of the band.

In the front hall, we slipped our row houses over our heads and stood side by side, checking ourselves out in the Whites' huge full-length mirror. Sarah asked her mom to take our picture, then ran to the kitchen for bags to hold our candy.

We left the house as soon as the streetlights went on, kicking our way through the leaves on the front lawn, then joined the stream of walkers on the sidewalk: the parents with infants out for their first Halloween, preschoolers dressed like cartoon characters, teenagers wearing garbage bags.

After just half an hour, our bags were getting heavy, so we returned to Sarah's house and took a break on the front steps. We lifted off our row houses and leaned them against the railings. We were swapping candy (her Snickers for my Skittles—a no-brainer as far as I was concerned) when two HCD seventh-grade girls walked up. Becca and Bella. Sarah knew them both from the neighborhood and from camp, the same camp she'd gone to with Blair.

Becca and Bella were dressed kind of like cheerleaders but with ghoulish green makeup, black wigs, and streaks of blood painted on their necks.

"Hey," Becca said.

"Hey," Sarah said.

"What are your costumes?" Becca asked, looking down at our fleeces and jeans.

"Oh, we're just resting," Sarah said. She stood up and reached for her row house costume, so I did too, and we stood side by side. "This is Genie," she added.

"Cool costumes," Bella said. "They must have taken a lot of time."

"What are you guys?" Sarah asked.

"Oh, we're like zombie cheerleaders or something," Becca said. "We totally did not know what to be until, like, three o'clock today. It was hilarious."

"We got the cheerleader costumes from school," Bella added. "The rest we just did whatever—crazy hair, crazy makeup. And we were, like, well, I guess we're cheerleaders, but zombified!"

"Zombified!" Becca said, wrapping her hands around Bella's neck.

"Zombified!" Bella echoed, pretending to strangle Becca.

A white car pulled up, driven by an older girl. A younger girl got out. She was wearing bright, sparkly makeup and teetering around on high-heeled shoes. I didn't think I knew her, but then I recognized her outfit: a minidress the color of a traffic cone.

"Sare!" the girl said.

"Oh my God, Blair!" Sarah said. "You look awesome!"

"You like? I'm an eighties rock star," Blair said, spinning around.

The white car pulled away.

"So awesome!" Becca and Bella said. "Oh my God, this is better than when you dressed up as a zombie cat for the camp dance!"

"I thought you were in DC!" Sarah said.

"My parents had to fly out to Arizona at the last minute. My au pair just broke up with her boyfriend and is making me crazy. Can I spend the night at your house?"

"Sure," Sarah said.

A couple of seventh-grade boys dressed like lacrosse players called out to Becca and Bella and headed our way. They looked at Blair in her rock-star outfit, then walked off with Becca and Bella.

"Did you see those guys checking me out?" Blair asked.

"Yeah," Sarah said.

Blair pulled out her cell phone. "I'm gonna text Marta to let her know I'm spending the night."

Marta was the au pair, I gathered. Until I met Blair I'd never even heard the term *au pair*. Apparently it means a teenager from another country who lives with a family and babysits.

A mother walked by with twin toddler girls dressed as ladybugs. "Oh my gosh," she said to Sarah and me.

"What unique costumes! So creative! Can I take your picture?"

"Sure," I said and nudged Sarah, who, like Blair, had turned around completely to see where the seventh graders had gone. When Sarah turned back around, the mother snapped the photo.

"Should we keep going?" I asked. "I need to get more Twix for my dad."

"For your dad, huh?" Blair said, her voice as sharp as a paper cut.

"Yeah," I said. "For my dad."

Blair turned to Sarah. "Can we just go inside and, like, watch a movie or something? I'm so *done* with the whole trick-or-treating thing."

Sarah said nothing for a moment, then turned to me: "We have Twix inside. We'll get some for your dad, okay, Genie?"

"Okay," I said. I dropped back behind Sarah and Blair as we walked through the front door into the house. There really wasn't room for three.

CHAPTER 7

Dream Journals

In the next science class, Ms. Kim started a unit about sleep and dreams. We talked about the stages of sleep and why sleep is important for our brains and bodies. Then we watched a short movie showing a person in different stages of sleep. We got to see what the rapid eye movement of REM sleep looks like.

In the middle of class, Ms. Kim had to leave the room for a minute. While she was gone, Blair and Drew snuck over and put a round red thing on her chair. What was it? I asked Anna Miles, who whispered that it was a whoopee cushion. I had heard of whoopie pie in English, where we were learning about the Amish, but not whoopee cushions.

Ms. Kim returned. There were only ten minutes

left in class. I kept wondering whether she was going to sit down at her desk. We all kept looking at each other while she was talking.

"What is going on, guys?" Ms. Kim finally asked. "Did someone tape a funny note on my back?"

My face had already felt pink. Now it felt red.

Ms. Kim looked at the blackboard, then under the classroom tables. She went behind her desk and pulled out her desk chair. "Aha! Very kind. Thank you for this lovely present, class. Now let's move on."

Blair and Drew looked at each other with raised eyebrows.

꒰ꂓ꒱ ꒰ꂓ꒱

Our assignment for the next week was to keep a dream journal, writing down at least four nights' worth of dreams. Ms. Kim told us to put a pad of paper beside our beds. Every time we woke up in the middle of the night or the first thing in the morning, we were supposed to write down what we had been dreaming about in as much detail as possible. Were we dreaming in color? What was happening? Who was in the dream? That sort of stuff. We would share our dream journals in class. We shouldn't feel foolish about our dreams, she said, because we couldn't control their content.

From Science we went straight to lunch. It was grilled cheese and applesauce—everyone's favorite.

"My mother told me that if you have a dream where you're not wearing all your clothes, that means you are ashamed about something in real life," Hassan said.

"Oh my God," Jack said, squirting mustard, ketchup, relish, mayonnaise, and syrup onto his grilled cheese, then eating it. (Would a girl ever try to gross people out like this?) "I have those *all* the time."

"Blair has a lot of those too!" Sarah said.

"Really?" Drew said.

"Sare Bear!" Blair squealed as she started tickling Sarah. Blair's elbow knocked Sarah's milk carton over. Both were giggling.

I went to get extra napkins and clean up the mess.

⌒⊙) (⊙⌒

In study hall that afternoon, Sarah passed me a note. I read it, then wrote on it and passed it back.

The year before, Sarah had started using hearts instead of dots under question marks and exclamation points and using circles to dot her *i*'s. It caught on

Mom said I can have you over Friday night. Can you come?

yes!

with almost every girl in the class. The only time we were not allowed to use them was on real school papers that would go home to our parents.

In carpool, Sarah and I planned what to do at our sleepover. We would have to spend a little time playing Girlz dolls with Nora, who always thought our sleepovers were for her too. Sarah had the MoveMania Fit game that I'd been saving up for, so we'd definitely do that. Then we'd eat dinner (the Whites always had the best dinners). Nora would go to bed, and then Sarah and I would be free to do whatever we wanted.

We'd probably just watch some movies and hang out.

"What kind of food do you girls want for your playdate?" Mrs. White asked us.

"Mom!" Sarah shouted. "The word is not 'playdate.' We're in fifth grade!"

"Okay, okay, I forgot! What kind of food do you girls want for your *sleepover*?"

"Mimo's Pizza," said Sarah. "Not Shane's. Blair says their kitchen is SO filthy." My family got pizza from Shane's sometimes. I thought it was okay, but apparently Blair didn't.

"Yeah, pizza would be great," I said, trying to sound nicer than Sarah sounded. Sarah always spoke a lot more politely to other people's parents than she did to her mom.

⌒)(⌒

Dream journal week fell right into the Wishes, Hopes, and Dreams blog theme, so I obviously had to blog about it, right?

Dream Journal Week

Don't forget to write down your dreams this week!
Remember that Ms. Kim said not to feel foolish.
It's not like you have any control over what you
dream!

I read more about dreams on a Web site
tonight. Some of the most common dreams
involve flying, falling, being attacked, and having
your teeth fall out. Also, there are dreams where
you're missing a piece of clothing and feeling
ashamed (Jack?).

Wish #4: That no one dreams of being chased
into the ocean by an angry octopus the size of an
elephant. (Not that I ever have . . .)

....

ANNA MILES This is going to be too embarrassing.

....

MACY I know!

....

JACK It's an honor just to be mentioned.

....

ANNA MILES Genie, can you grant me a wish? I'd like to be absent that day.

∽◌) (◌∽

On Friday night, Sarah, Nora, and I had a great time playing with Girlz dolls and MoveMania. We worked up a sweat in the dance segment, then had Italian ices. Nora was more fun to be with than usual, maybe because she was getting older.

Around seven o'clock, Blair called. She talked so loudly, I could hear her through the receiver. She wanted to know what Sarah was up to. Then she said that she was waiting to leave for some "stupid party" with her parents. I sighed, relieved that we wouldn't be repeating our Halloween-night threesome.

After Nora went to bed, Sarah and I lay down, each of us on our own sofa, to watch TV. The sofas were new and covered with the same kind of buttery leather as Rebecca's mom's gloves, the ones I'd held the night of the parents' cocktail party.

I was so sleepy, I thought I might slip right off the sofa. It wouldn't have hurt if I had. The room's carpeting was so soft, you almost bounced when you walked on it. I knew that the Persian rugs Gran loved were supposed to be attractive, but they didn't bounce, not even a little bit.

"Do you think Drew likes Blair?" Sarah asked.

"I guess," I said, shrugging my shoulders.

"No, I mean *likes* likes."

"I don't know." Honestly, I'd never thought about it. This whole way of using "like" had appeared in our class out of nowhere this year. I was still getting used to it.

"Blair's so fun," Sarah said. "She was the coolest person at camp. Don't you think she's cool?"

"Yeah," I said, but my voice sounded flat, like soda that had lost all its fizz.

CHAPTER 8

Family Day

On Sunday morning, two days after my sleepover with Sarah, I dreamed I was in the cafeteria with Sarah and Blair, but I had forgotten to wear pants. I kept trying to cover up, worried that someone would notice. Then Mr. Sayler came over to talk to me. He had a normal head but a sparrow's body. We stood there, staring at each other, me half-dressed and my teacher half-bird.

Mr. Sayler, the sparrow!

I woke up with a dry mouth and hot cheeks creased by the pillow. Before going downstairs, I went to the bathroom and held a cold washcloth to my face for a minute. It had been such a weird dream. I couldn't get Mr. Saylerbird out of my head.

In the kitchen I found Dad scrambling eggs, toasting challah bread (his favorite), and listening to NPR. He sipped coffee with his left hand while he stirred the eggs with his right. "Good morning, sunshine!" he said.

"Hi," I said.

We heard Ian on the steps. Dad looked at me with raised eyebrows and handed me my plate of food. It was rare for Ian to appear before ten on a weekend.

"Howdy, sunshine," Dad said to Ian in his Texas-cowboy accent. I laughed.

"Dad, you're a dork," Ian said. He looked at me. "You too."

I'm not sure how it happened exactly or who proposed the idea, but Ian and Dad and I decided to hang out together that day, just the three of us. I was going to skip church. Dad called a friend to sub for him in the MAC gallery, where he'd been scheduled to work all afternoon.

I went upstairs to get dressed. I even put on a little of this Recherché perfume that was my mother's. I kept it on top of the dresser next to a tiny photo of the two of us taken on the day that she and Dad brought me home from the hospital. This part of the dresser was kind of my Mom shrine.

Ian, Dad, and I piled into Dad's car. We drove by some outdoor sculptures at MAC, then stopped at the Walters Art Museum to see a new exhibit. At lunch, I asked Ian what a whoopee cushion did. He laughed and said he couldn't believe I had gotten to fifth grade without knowing what a whoopee cushion was. Dad told him to cut to the chase.

"Okay," Ian said. "You put them on people's chairs when they're not looking, and then they sit down."

"And?" I said.

Then he reached under his T-shirt and made a

huge farting sound with his underarm, and everyone in the restaurant zapped their heads around to look at our table, and I waited to die from embarrassment.

In the early evening, after Gran left for dinner with a friend, I took Dad's laptop into the living room and sat on the sofa next to Dad and Ian, who were watching a video that some of Ian's friends had made. It was time for a new blog post.

Don't Forget!

Don't forget to bring in your dream journals tomorrow. We all want to hear what your subconscious has to say!

Wish #5: That Ms. Kim has been keeping a dream journal too.

. . . .

ANNA MILES Here's what my subconscious says: "Please don't make me!"

BLAIR My dreams have been totally R-rated this week! Just ask Sarah!

DREW Need deets.

BLAIR No way!!!!!!!!!!!!!!!!!!!!!!!

DREW I will get it out of you one way or another. Or Sarah.

BLAIR Ooooh I'm sooo skeeeered!!!!!!!!!!!!!

SARAH Me too!

DREW You should be.

BLAIR LOL!!

DREW Here I come.

BLAIR Eeeeeek!!!!!!

··

MR. SAYLER Guys, the class blog isn't the place for
an extended personal conversation—
if in fact that's what you'd call this.

Dad read over my shoulder. "Who are Drew and
Blair?"

"Drew is Sarah's cousin, and Blair's this new girl
who went to camp with Sarah."

"What's Blair like?"

"She's okay."

"Oooh," Ian said. "Is she, like, trying to *steal Sarah
away*?"

"Shut up," I said. "Dad, can we pleeeeaaaase do
a Soulmates profile for you?" It must have been the
twentieth time I'd asked that question.

"Okay," Dad said.

"Okay?" I squealed.

"Let's get it over with," Dad said.

Ian raised an eyebrow. "Soulmates, Dad? How
lame is that?"

"Ian!" I said. "C'mon!"

"It doesn't hurt to try things," Dad said.

"All right, then, time for me to get out of here," Ian said, heading for the stairs. He went up halfway, then came back down and pointed at Dad. "Do not, under any circumstances, reveal that you're a lepidopterist!" He disappeared back up the stairs.

"A what?" I asked.

"Someone who studies moths and butterflies," Dad said, "which I'm not, but apparently he likes the word."

Dad and I went through hundreds of profile questions. Did he like sushi or pizza better? Late nights of dancing or quiet evenings at home? Old houses with character, or new construction?

"Sushi, quiet evenings, old houses. Geez, I sound like a total bore," Dad said. "Why do I have to choose just one of everything?"

"They have a formula for matching people. It works. Fifty percent of people who meet on this site go out on at least three dates together."

"And how did you become such an expert?"

"I watch the commercials. Here's another question. 'As a boyfriend, are you more like a high-speed express train running between cities or a historic steam train winding along a scenic coastline?' What does that mean?"

"I refuse to even answer that," he said.

"I guess that's okay," I said, skipping to the next question.

In the last step, we uploaded his profile photo, using the photo from his faculty Web page. He was wearing the brown tweed sportcoat and button-down shirt that he'd worn to the parents' cocktail party.

I didn't think it was the best picture he could have chosen. He wasn't even look-ing at the camera, and his face was sad. But he liked it because he was standing in front of one of his favorite buildings in Baltimore.

"Don't tell Gran about this Soulmates thing yet," he said. "Let's just keep it between you and me—and Ian, I guess."

"Okay," I said.

"I don't mean to sound like I don't appreciate your help, because I do," he said. "Thanks for helping me get off my duff." He kissed me on the top of the head and left the room.

Who would Dad's soul mate be? I couldn't wait to find out.

CHAPTER 9

Beating Heart

The next morning, I woke up from a dream about being on the beach in San Diego. I went there in real life once, during the summer after first grade, when Dad had taken Ian and me to see where Mom had grown up. The shallow part of the water stretched far out into the ocean, so that even as a first grader I could walk and walk and still have the blue-violet water come up only to my knees.

In my dream, I was standing by myself in the shallow water holding a baby. Whose baby, I didn't know. Everything fit together, everything was calm: the air, the water, the baby, and me. It was a lot nicer than my half-naked cafeteria dream with Mr. Saylerbird. Finally, something to write about in my dream journal!

After getting dressed, I checked Dad's Soulmates .com profile. He was a hit! Women had left winks all over his page. There were ten messages in his in-box. "Dad!" I shrieked. "Come look!"

Dad was just coming back from the shower, rubbing his wet head with a towel. He glanced at the screen. "Mmm," he said.

"Read them!"

"In a bit," he said.

When I got to Mr. Sayler's room, Blair was sitting on top of her desk with Sarah, Rebecca, and a few other girls fanned out around her, giggling. The room hummed. I noticed that Anna Miles had come in after all, despite her embarrassment.

"Sorry your wish didn't come true," I said to her.

In fourth period, Ms. Kim got straight to the heart of the matter: "As you all know, dream journal day has arrived. I'm very interested in hearing not only what your dreams were like but also what you think they might mean. Would anyone like to start?"

Rebecca waved her arm. "Okay, well I had this dream that I was with Genie? We were riding bikes on these winding, hilly roads and finally we got to a lake and stopped to rest and then I looked and Genie all of a sudden was my father instead—isn't that funny how Genie turned into my father? I don't know why—and anyway we got back on the bikes and we kept riding and then I woke up, I think?"

Sometimes when I tried to tell my dreams to Gran, she would correct me on my grammar and suggest that I pause for a sentence break once in a while, and by the time she reminded me of all that stuff, I usually lost interest in telling her my dream at all.

"What did you notice about how the world looked in the dream?" Ms. Kim asked Rebecca. "Were the images very vivid? Were they in color?"

"I remember that the trees were a bright green? It felt like a really long dream? I have no idea what it meant, though?"

Other people mentioned dreams about things at home and things at school, outdoor things and indoor things, family members and friends. Camels, polka-dot minivans, tunnels covered in blue slime. We talked about possible dream meanings and how the dreams made us feel.

As we neared the end of class, Rebecca piped up with a question: "Did you keep a journal, Ms. Kim? Genie was hoping you might have."

"Ha! No," said Ms. Kim.

Jack raised his hand. "I had a dream with Sarah in it."

"Of course you did!" Blair said.

"Don't interrupt," Ms. Kim said, putting a finger to her lips. "So what happened in the dream?"

"We went to see a movie, only it turned out that it was not the movie we planned to see. It was some movie about dinosaurs. And then the dinosaurs started coming off the screen and into the theater and eating everybody's popcorn. Weird, huh?"

"Interesting," Ms. Kim said. "You guys have very

creative dream minds. Now head off to lunch! Class dismissed."

~ゐ) (ঌ~

At lunch, Blair and Sarah couldn't stop talking about Jack's dream. Jack kept looking over at our table. Finally, Blair shouted over to him. "It's really obvious that you like Sarah. You should ask her out."

Sarah hid her face in her hands.

My family would never let me go on a date in fifth grade, but not all families were like mine. Would Sarah's parents actually let her go on a date this year?

Blair turned to me. "How come we never hear about *your* crushes?"

"I don't have any," I said.

"How is that, like, even *possible*?"

"Blair!" Rebecca protested.

"You don't have a crush on *anyone*?"

"Okay, there is this one guy in my neighborhood," I said.

"Really?" Sarah asked.

"What does he look like?" Blair asked.

"He's got blond hair and blue eyes and he's . . . funny."

"What's his name?" Blair asked.

"Lucas." It was the first name I could think of.

Okay, so I made up a crush.

I looked over at Anna Miles, who was sitting with Sophie and Macy, drawing a real heart—the kind you'd see in a science book. Macy was watching intently as she finished her chocolate pudding, which was making a mess of her braces, but she didn't care.

∞◯) (◯∞

In carpool later, Sarah asked for more details about my crush. I told her there really wasn't much else to say—I'd just seen him around the neighborhood. I could have told her the truth, but then she might have told Blair, and the conversation I hadn't felt like having in the first place would just begin again.

When I got home, I logged on to Dad's Soulmates account and saw that he'd set up a date with this one woman after work. As soon as he came home that night, I ran up the stairs behind him. "I saw it!" I whispered.

"What?"

"The date notice! The date scheduler! You had a date!"

"Yes," he laughed. "I did."

"So, where did you go?"

"Wait a second." He walked into the bathroom, then got dressed for bed. His knees looked especially knobby beneath his slouchy pajama shorts, and his hair was damp and tufted, like a disoriented bird's. "We met at that coffee place near the Walters Art Museum."

"And what was she like?"

"Um, she writes film reviews for the *Harbor News*, that free weekly paper. She lives in a condo downtown. She has two dogs."

"What kind of dogs?"

"I forget."

"Do you like her? Were you nervous?"

"I think I like her. I was kind of nervous, yeah. And now I'm wiped out—gotta get to bed."

Dad, nervous? He never got nervous, not about teaching classes or giving artists' talks or anything.

I thought about Anna Miles's sketch again, and it struck me that a real heart—not the line-drawn valentine kind but the living, beating variety—looked like a sea creature just plucked from its shell, glistening and fragile.

CHAPTER 10

Field Trip

Thanksgiving was quiet, just the four of us and Uncle Mike, my father's younger brother. Uncle Mike lived about an hour north of us and sold mortgages or something, but if you asked him what he did for a living, he'd say he was an inventor. He always carried a notepad and pen in his shirt pocket, in case a new idea struck him. I liked hanging out with Uncle Mike.

∽◦)) ((◦∽

In English the week after Thanksgiving, we finished *Shoofly Pie and Other Tales*, a book of stories about kids born into Amish families in Lancaster County, Pennsylvania. The kids in the stories did lots of farmwork and lived in communities that were very religious. They wore plain, old-fashioned clothes and didn't use electricity from power lines or drive motorized cars. Our English teacher, Mrs. Hanson, said that because we finished the book early, she would arrange a field trip to Lancaster County, where we could visit an Amish farm market.

We had a small English class, just eight kids—the "top readers," Mrs. Hanson called us when she forgot she wasn't supposed to say things like that. At ten in the morning on Wednesday we all piled into her mini-van. We almost had to leave without Sam, who had forgotten his permission slip, but at the last minute his mom dropped it off. We were crammed in kind of tightly, with every seat belt taken, and Hassan, who was the tallest, had to sit up front in the passenger seat. I was sitting in the back between Sophie and Walker, a boy from the other homeroom who I didn't know very well but who was almost as funny as Jack.

I couldn't believe how messy the van was. You could tell Mrs. Hanson had pushed some stuff under the seats so that we'd all have a place. We had the windows open, and the air was soft and warm for December, but when we got on the highway, the wind started gusting through the car, kicking up gum wrappers and other trash.

Everyone cheered when we crossed the state line into Pennsylvania. When we got onto the back roads, we started seeing farms and road signs showing horses pulling buggies.

(Was I the only ten-year-old girl in America who couldn't draw a horse? My horse looked more like two people wearing a horse costume.)

"Those signs let cars know that there are Amish buggy drivers sharing these roads. It keeps everyone safer," Mrs. Hanson said.

"The buggies are going, like, two miles an hour. How can that not be safe?" Hassan asked.

"If they were the only things on the road, it would be fine, but when you have other vehicles whooshing by these buggies, problems start," said Mrs. Hanson.

Mrs. Hanson seemed like a pretty good driver, even if her car was messy.

∘৹◗) (◖৹∘

The Amish farm market was huge and bright and decorated for Christmas, which was only a few weeks away. We all stayed in our group. Our first stop was the bakery, where tables were lined with cakes and pies. We saw shoofly pie, which we had read about. It was full of molasses and brown sugar and was supposed to be very sweet. We also saw whoopie pies,

 which were sandwiches of cake filled with thick white frosting.

We spent a few minutes each at the cheese counter, the deli counter, and the produce area, then sat in the restaurant to eat. The nine of us took up two booths. Sophie and I sat on one side of a corner booth, and Sam and Hassan on the other. Behind the boys was a wall painted to look like the outdoors, with rolling green farmland and red covered bridges.

Sophie and I talked about television shows we liked while Hassan and Sam talked about video games and

Legos. Then the waitress came to our table. Hassan ordered a veggie burger, Sophie and I got cheeseburgers, and Sam ordered a patty melt. He had never had one, he said. None of us had either.

When the food came, he was totally disappointed. The patty melt looked like a grilled cheese, but on rye bread, with hamburger. His face fell. We all offered to share our food, but he wouldn't take any.

Mrs. Hanson squatted down at the end of our booth. She asked how our lunches were, and everyone except Sam said lunch was good.

"So, class blogger, are you going to blog about this field trip?" she asked.

"Probably," I said. Now that she mentioned it, it was a good idea.

Hassan whispered something to Sam, then laughed really hard.

"Something you'd like to share, boys?" Mrs. Hanson asked.

"Nope," Hassan said.

"I wonder whether Junk Food Lunch will ever come

back," Sophie said. "Like you wished in that first post."

"Rebecca would be so happy," I said.

"Me too!" Sophie said.

"I read that post," Mrs. Hanson said. "It was fine, but if you *really* want to get anywhere with the idea, you probably should write a more persuasive post. *Why* should Junk Food Lunch come back? How does it benefit the school or the students? There's nothing wrong with wishing, but you need to flesh out your argument."

Argument seemed like a strong word. "I don't think I'm supposed to use the blog to argue," I said.

"I don't mean *argue* in the sense of being disagreeable. I mean *argue* in the sense of building your case, the way a lawyer might. Let's call it persuasive wishing. Maybe we could work on it together in English class sometime."

Persuasive wishing, I thought. Huh.

∞◐) (◑∞

After lunch we walked around some more, looking at the furniture and candy areas. The teenagers working at the stalls looked like how I had pictured them in *Shoofly Pie.* The boys had short, rounded haircuts, and their pants were held up by suspenders. The girls had long hair that was pulled back tightly into buns, and they wore head coverings and plain dresses. They seemed like people who had time traveled to the twenty-first century. I knew not to stare, but there was so much I wanted to see.

"It's pretty cool here, huh?" Sophie said. "I mean different, but cool."

"Yeah," I said, looking at our group. We didn't even have to wear uniforms for school, much less for life in general. Sophie had on jeans. Sam had hair down to his shoulders and a T-shirt with a surfing mouse on it. Hassan had neat, ironed clothes, but even he looked almost disheveled next to the Amish kids. Compared with them, we were all kind of boisterous, ping-ponging around their market stalls. What were the Amish kids thinking of *us*?

Before leaving, we stopped at the soft-pretzel counter and each got a pretzel to take in the car.

Hardly anyone talked on the drive home. We all just sat on the upholstered seats, staring out the windows.

We pulled into the school parking lot not long before dismissal. When I got to Mr. Sayler's room, Blair and Sarah were wedged into Sarah's desk chair, watching something on Blair's phone.

"Where were you?" Blair asked.

"Field trip for English," I said.

"Oh right. What did Drew call it?" Blair said. "Geeks on the Go. Was it like geek heaven, having all of you in one car?" Her laugh shot out sharply, like a spring tightly coiled, then released.

After I finished helping with the dinner dishes that night, Gran called me into the living room to look at her laptop, where her browser was open to a blog titled Eve's Reads. "Eve is the granddaughter of a college friend of mine. She started out reviewing kids' books, but she's expanded to blog about other things—life in general. She's got quite a following, and she's only a couple of years older than you."

I went to Dad's computer and pulled up the Eve's Reads blog. Eve talked about things that were going on between her friends in her seventh-grade class and in the world—good and bad things both. She asked her readers big questions—and they answered in the comments. Eve was funny but also serious in places.

As I went to write my blog post that night, I felt different. The feeling was hard to explain. Between going to the Amish market, talking to Mrs. Hanson about persuasive wishing, and reading Eve's blog, my mind felt bigger, like it was taking up more space than it had before.

Field Trip

Today my English class went to Lancaster County, Pennsylvania, to see the area we had been reading about in a book called *Shoofly Pie and Other Tales*. It was pretty interesting. What

I thought was coolest about the Amish was that even though they don't use a lot of the modern stuff we have, and they live in an old-fashioned kind of way, they seem totally happy. Do the Amish kids have the same kinds of wishes, hopes, and dreams we have? Probably.

Wish #6: That we go on more field trips this year and in middle school.

....

SAM — Yes, but do not order patty melts. Ever.

....

SOPHIE — It was fun hanging out w/ you, Genie! :)

....

BLAIR — I would DIE if I had to be Amish. Boring!!!!

I saw Blair's comment, then closed the lid on Dad's laptop. I might be trying to reach farther in my blog posts, the way Eve did, but that didn't mean everybody would respond the way I wanted them to.

CHAPTER 11

Wrap Party

Jn early December, not long after the field trip, my classmate Josh's mom came in to talk about Hanukkah with us. We all got dreidels and ate latkes, and she explained the origins of the holiday and the significance of the menorah. She started to tell a funny story about Josh's first Hanukkah, but Josh said "Mom!" as soon as his mother got to the word *diaper*.

After we'd finished the latkes and cleaned up, Josh's mom left, and Mr. Sayler took us to the art room. The whole lower school had been collecting new toys to give to a homeless shelter for the holidays, and as fifth graders, the oldest in the lower school, we got to wrap and deliver the gifts. Today was the wrap party.

Mr. Sayler had set up workstations around the room, each with a thick tube of holiday wrapping paper, tape, and several pairs of scissors. Sarah, Rebecca, and I went to the station at the far corner of the room. Blair followed.

Soon, the room was alive with holiday sounds: scissors slicing through paper, fingers squeaking along folds, and tape being ripped from dispensers. You could almost smell the pine trees. Christmas was so soon!

Rebecca and I each wrapped small board games while Blair and Sarah tried to wrap a sled. Half the time they were turned around on their stools, talking to Drew, Hassan, and Jack at the next table.

When Blair and Sarah were finally done, the sled looked as if it had been wrapped by toddlers. Apparently, it was hard to wrap and flirt at the same time.

A few minutes later, while I was wrapping a video game, Rebecca screamed and leaped up, her metal stool screeching against the linoleum.

"What happened?" Sarah asked.

Rebecca's face was red. "Nothing," she said, but she ran over to Mr. Sayler and they left the room. Everyone strained to hear their hallway conversation through the open door.

"What happened?" Sarah whispered to me.

I shrugged my shoulders.

Then Hassan, Drew, and Jack were called out into the hall. Ms. Miller, the school counselor, joined the group too.

About five minutes later, Mr. Sayler came to the door. "Okay, everyone, finish up whatever you're working on, and let's go back to the classroom."

"What about the rest of the presents?" Blair asked.

"Whoever's staying for after-school care today can finish wrapping them with me," Mr. Sayler said. "Just leave everything where it is."

As we filed behind him down the hall, past the banner that said "Respect," he rubbed the top of his bald head, as if for luck.

"We need to talk about what happened a few minutes ago," Mr. Sayler said once we'd all settled back into our desks. "Ms. Miller, the floor is yours."

Ms. Miller stood up and adjusted her headband, which was pink with green alligators on it. "Hi, every-one. I just want to clear the air a little bit about what happened today. You are all getting older, and your bodies are changing, as you know. Everyone's body matures at a different rate. We'll be talking about this when we get back from winter break, in health class."

A couple of people groaned.

"I know some of you have heard about health class from older brothers and sisters," Ms. Miller contin-ued, "and let me tell you, it's not as bad as they make it out to be. They love telling you their war stories. But I promise, each and every one of you will survive it.

"In the meantime, what I'd really like to remind you is that puberty"—more groans, since no one in our class liked this word—"is not something to tease each other about. Give each other the space to change and grow. Change and grow. That's really all I wanted to say."

"Thanks, Ms. Miller," Mr. Sayler said. "Well, guys, it's kinda late. Why don't you just get out your pleasure-reading books and read quietly until carpool." He went out into the hallway with Ms. Miller.

The talk was over, but we still hadn't gotten to the heart of the matter.

Sarah wrote "What happened????" on a piece of paper and passed it to Rebecca.

Rebecca wrote on the paper, then passed it back to Sarah, who showed it to me. "Drew snapped the back of my bra," it said. Rebecca had gotten her first training bra a few days earlier.

The dreaded snapping? The thing that Blair had mentioned at Sarah's slumber party back in October? It had finally started.

I looked at Drew, who had his head planted in a book. By the way he looked, you'd think that *How to Talk to Your Unicorn* was the best book he'd ever read. I knew it wasn't, because I'd read it. It wasn't even good.

After school that day, when I was still thinking hard about what had happened to Rebecca, Ian came home with a scruffy little black dog he'd found in an alley. Her collar had "Lulu" embroidered on it, but she had no tags. She had a chocolate muzzle, jet-black eyes, and a very funny underbite. She had so much hair, it was hard to tell whether she was coming or going.

Ian put Lulu down on our living room floor, and she started sniffing the Persian rugs. Pretty soon she was going to the bathroom on one.

"Lulu!" Gran snapped.

Ian carried Lulu outside to the grass, then brought her back in.

"What kind of dog is she?" I asked.

"A mutt. Looks like she's part poodle, though," Ian said.

"She's so cute. Can we keep her?" I asked.

"First we have to see if she belongs to someone else," Ian said. He took a photo with Dad's cell phone, then went upstairs to his computer.

"Someone will probably call about her," Gran said.

"What if they don't?" I asked.

"Let's give it a few weeks," Gran said.

"A few weeks?" I said.

"Until Christmas," Dad said.

"Can she sleep in my bed? Please?" I asked Gran.

"Let's hold off until a vet has looked at her," said Gran.

That night, I sat at my dad's computer with Lulu in my lap, thinking about my blog post. I considered writing about the bra snapping, but how would that work? *Wish #7: That it doesn't happen again?* Would Eve write about that on Eve's Reads?

In the end, I decided to write about Lulu and the donated gifts instead.

Wishes

Isn't it weird how sometimes you wish for something and it actually comes true? Just a couple of weeks ago, I woke up really early and was bored and was wishing for someone to hang out with. Then today, my brother found a dog in our neighborhood. Her name's Lulu. If no one calls by Christmas, we can keep her forever. And in the meantime I've got someone to hang out with when I get up early. My wish came true, at least temporarily. Did anything like this ever happen to you guys?

I wonder what the kids we wrapped presents for today are hoping to get for the holidays. Probably all the same stuff we're hoping for, right?

Wish #7: That those kids and all of us too have a great holiday—maybe even a little snow?

....

JACK   One time I really wanted a goalie lacrosse stick, just to play with, and then this friend of my dad's had one he was getting rid of. It was cool.

....

ANNA MILES Last year, I hadn't mentioned to anyone that I wanted new drawing

pencils, but my dads gave me a set
for my birthday!

....

MACY   My mom says once you're an adult
you wish for abstract things (peace,
health, etc.) instead of toys and stuff,
and that's one way you know you've
grown up. I don't wish for things
a lot, because that way I'm never
disappointed.

....

JACK   Are you saying I need to GROW UP???
LOL.

....

ANNA MILES   Lulu sounds AWESOME!!

....

SARAH   I want to meet her!

CHAPTER 12

Secret Friend

After the wrap party, the couple of weeks until HCD's winter break were basically one long celebration punctuated by occasional tests. I wondered how the custodians would ever get all the sprinkles and sparkles out of the classroom rugs.

During the last week before vacation, we always had a secret-gift exchange. It had once been called Secret Santa, but a couple of years ago the school had renamed it Secret Friend.

On Monday we drew classmates' names out of a hat. On Wednesday you were supposed to give your friend a small present (three dollars or under). Thursday was for homemade things. Friday was the big present (something under ten dollars).

Secret Friend Week!

Secret Friend is one of the best traditions at HCD—possibly even better than Junk Food Lunch (which we're still hoping will return, by the way).

Remember that Mr. Sayler's not going to set aside special time for people to get their presents to their Secret Friends. You'll just have to find a way to deliver them, even if it means coming into school early or handing the present off to someone else to deliver for you. We're pretty lucky to go to a school where the lockers have no locks! It makes Secret Friend gift delivery a lot easier.

Wish #8: That all of us keep the names we drew a secret! (It makes Secret Friend more fun.)

....

JACK   Should I get you that MoveMania game you're always talking about?

....

JACK   Oops. I mean . . . maybe I'm your SF, maybe I'm not. Darn it, why can't I delete a comment?!

SARAH Duh! Way to keep your cover!

REBECCA R.I.P., Junk Food Lunch. I fear you are never coming back. :(

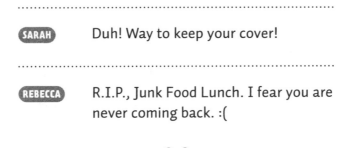

On Monday night, Gran took me to Emporia, a huge store in the suburbs, to shop for Sophie, whose name I had drawn. For Wednesday's present I found a key chain with a dog that looked like Lulu, and even though Lulu wasn't Sophie's dog (or my dog either, technically, yet), I still thought Sophie would like the key chain. Thursday's present was easy. We had so many cookies at our house (Gran had baked dozens and dozens), I would give Sophie a tin of those. Friday I was having a harder time with, but Gran said that tonight was our only chance to get to a store, so I found a pair of sparkly earrings that looked like tiny distant stars and cost only $8.99. Sophie was lucky; she already had pierced ears.

I wasn't allowed to get my ears pierced until I was twelve.

On Wednesday I found a miniature flashlight perched on the top shelf of my locker. At the bottom of my locker lay a piece of scrap paper that said "Your Secret Friend."

On Thursday morning I opened the lid of my desk and found a carved duck no bigger than a bar of soap sitting on the pencil ledge. The duck was made out of a light wood, and you could still see the knife marks from the carving. The rough texture looked like feathers. It was hard to imagine that Jack had given me this.

 He didn't seem like someone who'd have the patience for whittling.

Meanwhile, Sarah had been getting crazy-nice stuff, way over the price limits and outside the day's gift guidelines. On Wednesday she got a twenty-five-dollar gift card to Anthropologie. On Thursday there was a whole makeup kit from a department store. Whose parents would let them buy all that?

At Friday's Secret Friend party, we had holiday cookies (still more sprinkles!) and soda. School was letting out at noon, since winter break was starting. Sarah was going home with Blair, and I was going home with Gran. I had the box with Sophie's earrings hidden in my pocket, and a few minutes into the party I walked up to her.

"Hey, Genie," she said, chewing on a bright green cookie.

"Hey," I said, pulling the box out of my pocket. She looked at it, and her eyes lit up.

"Are you my Secret Santa? I mean, Friend?"

"Yep," I said.

"Cool!" She put her cookie down on a napkin, took the box, and unwrapped it. When she saw the earrings, she squealed a little.

Blair walked up to Sarah holding a shiny blue gift bag and smiling.

"Oh my God!" Sarah said. "You? I totally can't believe it!" She gave Blair a big hug and opened the gift bag, which had a new Abercrombie & Fitch hoodie in it.

"I had to trade with two people to get you!" Blair said.

I was silently counting all the ways Blair had violated Secret Friend rules when I felt a tap on my shoulder. It was Jack.

"Hey, class blogger," Jack said.

"Hi," I said.

"I guess you're pretty sure I'm your Secret Friend."

"I don't know," I said.

"Well, I'm not!" he said, stepping aside. Sam was behind him, looking big and nervous and holding a warehouse-sized package of Milk Duds. He handed it to me.

"I hope you like them. I wasn't sure."

"Thanks," I said.

"See you next year," he said. He turned around and walked away. I looked at Sophie, and she cracked a smile.

Since Sarah and her hundred dollars' worth of Secret Friend presents were going home with Blair, I pulled on my parka, strapped on my backpack, gathered up my tub of Duds, and walked to the library to find my grandmother.

CHAPTER 13

Christmas

few days before Christmas, long after I'd handed Sam's tub of Milk Duds off to Ian, Dad and I were taking Lulu on a walk into Sarah's neighborhood. We were talking about Margo, the woman he'd met on Soulmates .com. They'd been going out pretty regularly, and he seemed happy. I hoped that Margo had not noticed the less-great things about Dad, like his knobby knees.

I had an idea: "Why don't you invite Margo to Christmas dinner?"

"No, it's too soon."

"But it would be fun! What's she doing for Christmas?"

"She's Jewish. I don't think she has big plans."

"Well, then she should *definitely* come!"

Dad laughed. "Well, okay, I guess. I'll ask her."

Christmas Eve at our house meant going to the family service at church (where my youth choir sang—pretty badly, I have to say) and having soup and bread for dinner. Before we went to bed every year, we put out beer and oranges for Santa. It was a tradition, and there was no reason not to do it, even as Ian and I got older.

Before I went to bed that night, I wrapped some sand tarts inside a napkin to take up to my room. Gran always said that sand tarts were just a dolled-up sugar cookie, but they were my favorite part of Christmas: all butter and sugar and cinnamon, with a slice of almond in the middle. The diamond-shaped ones always tasted best. I didn't know why.

I held the package of cookies against my chest with my left hand and patted my leg with my right hand. "Lulu!" I said. "Bedtime!"

Lulu bounded to my side, tongue wagging. Once we were upstairs, I'd break off a piece of sand tart for her.

No one had called about Lulu, so she was officially ours! I could tell she belonged in our family, because she liked sand tarts just as much as the rest of us. Every time I ate one, she would sit patiently, hoping for a piece to fall. Gran loved her too, especially since Lulu had finally stopped going to the bathroom on the Persian rugs. According to the vet, she was probably a shih tzu–poodle mix. A shih-poo. To me she looked like a little black bear.

When I ran downstairs on Christmas morning at five, Lulu bouncing step-by-step behind me, I found the empty bottle of beer and the orange peels on the table. All of a sudden I remembered I'd never made a Christmas list. Was that because having Lulu felt like a great enough present already? It seemed funny that I—the Wishes, Hopes, and Dreams blogger—would have forgotten about my own wish list.

I squeezed the toe of my Christmas stocking to feel the orange that Gran always put there, then inspected the presents under the tree. No one else would be up for a couple of hours, so I lay on the sofa with Lulu and watched cartoons.

Then I typed up a blog post.

Xmas!

Merry Christmas, everybody, if you celebrate Christmas! Who's up? If my family would just wake up, I could find out what's in this red stocking with my name on it.

Wish #9: That Santa brings you everything you wished for.

....

ANNA MILES Merry Xmas!!! I'm waiting too! I don't think my dads are EVER going to get up! xoxoxo

BETHANY OMGOMGOMG I can't believe Xmas is finally here.

Around seven o'clock, Gran came downstairs, already dressed in her Christmas sweater and some pants. Dad followed a few minutes later in his robe.

"We have to get Ian," I said. "Can I wake him up?"

"Sure," Dad said.

I knocked on Ian's door a few times. No response. Finally, I turned the knob and went in. A lock of dark hair stuck out from under the covers. I nudged him.

"What?" he said, not even moving.

"It's Christmas!"

He groaned.

"I can't open any presents until you get up!"

"Okay," he said. "I'm coming."

I stood there, waiting.

"Go back downstairs," he said. "I. Will. Be. There."

Besides the stuff in his stocking, Ian got a fifty-dollar iTunes card and a new winter coat. Dad and Gran gave me the MoveMania Fit game I'd been wanting forever. I couldn't believe it! Now I could use the money I'd been saving on something else.

I gave Dad and Gran framed copies of some fossil prints I'd done at school. Then I gave Ian a DVD of a skateboarding documentary that Dad had suggested he'd like.

Uncle Mike showed up for Christmas dinner around two o'clock. There was no suspense about his presents: he always gave Ian and me checks. I gave him the same fossil print I'd given Dad and Gran.

Fifteen minutes after Uncle Mike arrived, when Gran was down in the basement looking for more of her mother's embroidered Christmas napkins, the doorbell rang. Uncle Mike was closest, so he opened the door, holding the barking Lulu back with his foot. There stood a short woman with a huge poinsettia in her arms. I could hardly see her face behind the mass of leaves and petals.

Dad took the plant from Margo and kissed her on the cheek. Then Uncle Mike gave Margo a big bear hug. "So you're the lady who's captured my big brother's fancy!" he said. "I'm Mike. Will's the talented one, and I'm—well, the jury's still out on what I am."

Margo laughed. "Oh please," Dad said, shaking his head.

Next, Dad introduced Margo to Ian and me. Margo shook my hand, clasping one of her hands over the other, the way I'd seen the minister at church do it. She did the same with Ian.

Gran walked up from the basement, wiping her hands on her reindeer apron. She reached out to shake Margo's hand. "It's a pleasure to meet you. What a lovely plant. Thank you!"

"You're welcome," Margo said. "Thanks so much for inviting me."

"Can I offer you some tomato juice or maybe a glass of wine?"

"Some wine would be wonderful," Margo said.

We all went into the living room. Margo was so

short and her maroon skirt so long, it caught in the back of her heels as she walked.

As soon as Margo sat, Lulu jumped onto her lap. Lulu would probably do this with anybody, even a burglar, but still, it was nice to get our new dog's approval. Margo and Lulu had the same kind of hair—black and curly, flecked with silver.

Margo had presents for all of us: a silky scarf for Gran and knit ones for Dad and Ian, a year's subscription to *Tween Life* for me, and some homemade dog biscuits for Lulu. Lulu grabbed one biscuit, then hid behind the Christmas tree, the way she always did with things she really liked. Ian barely glanced at his new scarf before tossing it onto the piano bench. Dad gave him a look.

⤜◎) (◎⤛

A light snow began to fall during dinner, and the unexpected flurries made everyone extra happy (except Ian, who didn't seem very happy to begin with). A white Christmas was especially nice when it didn't interfere with holiday plans, Gran said. I smiled when I remembered wishing for holiday snow at the end of one of my blog posts. The wish had come true!

After dinner, I saw Dad and Margo talking out front, by her car. It looked as if she was shivering. Finally, they stopped talking, and Margo wrapped her arms around Dad's waist, and he leaned down and kissed the top of her head, and they just stood there like that, not saying anything, as the snowflakes fell onto them and stuck, as if they were plants or statues. They looked peaceful.

Ian walked up behind me and looked out the window. "Ugh. Gross," he said.

CHAPTER 14

Resolutions

round nine o'clock on the morning after Christmas, the phone rang. I ran to look at the caller ID but didn't recognize the number.

Gran picked up the handset. She always answered the phone, whether she recognized the number or not.

"Oh, hello, Sarah," she said, her voice suddenly shiny and bright, like tinsel. "Merry Christmas! Hold on a second. I'll get Genie."

"Hi!" I said. "Did you guys get a new number?"

"It's my new cell phone!" she said. "I got it for Christmas!"

"Cool," I said.

"Blair's been telling me what apps to download. What did you get for Christmas?"

"I got MoveMania."

"Cool!"

"Can you come over today?" I asked.

"I can't. I'm going skiing with Blair until New Year's Eve. We leave in a couple of hours. What are you up to?"

"Not much. Hanging out with my family mostly."

"Okay, well, I guess I'll see you back at school!"

"Okay, bye."

Sarah and I had always gotten together the day after Christmas to play with our gifts. Today she would be with Blair instead. I felt hollow—a feeling not even a roomful of diamond-shaped sand tarts could fix.

∽◯) (◯∽

In the end, the time between Christmas and New Year's Eve was fun. Here are some of the things I did:

❶ Saw two movies in a row with Uncle Mike and Ian at this new movie theater near Uncle Mike's house. Wondered whether we'd actually paid to see the second movie, so asked Uncle Mike, who said, "Shhhhh, the movie's starting."

❷ Saw one movie with Dad and Ian.

❸ Saw one movie with Dad and Margo. In French, with subtitles. Ian didn't want to go.

❹ Played MoveMania with Dad a lot.

❺ Played MoveMania with Ian once after promising I would never ask him to play it again.

❻ Played MoveMania by myself.

❼ Went to a church holiday party with Gran.

❽ Made two loaves of bread with Dad. One required kneading. One didn't. Took them to his friend's holiday party, where everyone decided the two loaves tasted the same.

❾ Went to the paint-your-own-ceramics place with Anna Miles and Macy. Tried to stay out of their huge fight about who was going to get to paint the last frog-shaped salt and pepper shakers in the store.

❿ Read through the past two years' worth of archived posts on Eve's Reads.

⑪ Read the entire Rachel Bixby series after hearing about it on Eve's Reads.

⑫ Decoupaged part of one bedroom wall with cool photos from magazines.

⑬ Ate seventy-five sand tarts (approximate).

⑭ Wrote captions for thirty pictures on Petzzz.com, where people post funny pictures of their pets sleeping. One of my cap- tions got sixty-three bones!

⤵) (⤴

On New Year's Eve, Dad and Margo went out to one party, and Ian went to another. Gran and I stayed home and were planning to watch *The Wizard of Oz*, eat popcorn dusted with Parmesan cheese, and drink sparkling apple cider.

"Where's Sarah been this week?" Gran asked as she pulled the popcorn out of the cupboard.

"Busy," I said. "She went skiing with Blair."

Gran looked at me. "She and Blair are pretty good friends, aren't they?"

"Yeah," I said. The hollow feeling had crept back in.

"You have lots of other friends too. Don't forget that."

"I know."

"I was talking to my college classmate—Eve's grandmother? She was thinking of bringing Eve down to Baltimore this spring, just for a day or two."

"That'd be great!" I said.

Meeting Eve? How cool would that be?

Around ten thirty, after Dorothy had returned to Kansas and Gran had shuffled off to bed, I went to Dad's computer and saw that Eve had posted a special edition of Eve's Reads called New Year's Eve's Reads. It contained all kinds of recommendations of books being released in the new year. Her blog was always so good.

I wondered whether Eve had ever read *my* blog. I

tried to imagine what it would look like through her eyes. Would it seem superficial? Immature? I hoped not.

New Year's Resolutions

My grandmother says resolutions are kind of like wishes, hopes, and dreams. Resolutions show how you hope to change in the future, and what kind of person you'd like to become. Even for a kid, this is important to think about, she says.

So here's mine: I'm resolving to take my new dog, Lulu (she's officially ours now!), on one long walk every day. My grandmother said I should resolve to clean my room once a week, but I like the Lulu resolution better, so I'm sticking with that one.

How about you guys? Do you have any resolutions?

Wish #10: That we all have a great new year!

ANNA MILES I can't believe you get to keep Lulu! That's so awesome!

SOPHIE Yay!

REBECCA Now I REALLY want to meet her!

SARAH Triple yay!!!!! And BTW my resolution is to do 30 sit-ups and 10 push-ups every day. I decided last night. Also, I need to learn to make cheesecake.

BLAIR Don't forget the diet, Sare Bear! You promised me we'd lose five pounds by spring vacation!

SARAH Oh yeah. Sorry, cheesecake. :(Have to go download the calorie app to my new smartphone!

MACY What? Phone? BTW, you guys are super-skinny already.

....

ANNA MILES Macy is soooooo right.

....

SARAH Xmas smartphone! Thx for being nice, but my butt is HUGE.

And just like that, we were back in a land of sit-ups and smartphones—Blair's world.

CHAPTER 15

Health Class

O n our first morning back from winter break, Mr. Sayler told us that for the next two days we'd be having health class after lunch instead of English. The girls would go with Ms. Miller and the boys with Mr. Pohler, the gym teacher.

At lunch Sarah was crowded into a table with Blair, Rebecca, Hassan, Jack, Drew, and a few other people. Sarah gestured for me to squeeze in next to her, but I said it was okay and went to the next empty table by myself.

Within a minute, Sophie had put her tray down next to mine, and Anna Miles and Macy had joined us. "Thanks again for the earrings," Sophie said. "I've been wearing them every day." She pointed to her ears.

"You're welcome," I said.

"You're not allowed to get your ears pierced yet?" Sophie asked.

"Not until I'm twelve."

"My mom is making me go to the doctor to get my ears pierced. She doesn't want to take any chances with infection," Macy said.

"Your mom worries about everything!" Anna Miles said.

"I know," Macy said.

Macy and Anna Miles had known each other since preschool, had a lot of sleepovers together, and took piano lessons with the same teacher. Sometimes they fought, but everyone knew they were best friends. It made me think of Sarah and me. Or, really, the way Sarah and I used to be. Were we still best friends?

"Oh my gosh," Macy whispered. "I meant to tell you over break—I saw what Sam gave you for Friday's Secret Friend gift!"

"I saw it too!" said Anna Miles. "Do you even like Milk Duds?"

"They're okay," I said.

"What did you do with them?" she asked.

"I gave them to Ian. He eats everything."

"Are you on a diet with Blair and Sarah?" Sophie asked.

"No, I just . . . you know, it's too much candy," I said. Even if Blair and Sarah *had* invited me to be on a diet with them, which they hadn't, my dad would have forbidden it. He always said that he hated to hear about little girls dieting.

Ms. Miller led us into her counseling office for health class. Though I'd walked by the office a million times, I'd never been inside. It was half the size of a classroom and not as brightly lit. The wall posters weren't math charts or photos of celebrities holding their favorite books—they were nature posters, with captions like "Let your dreams take flight!" My classmates and I scattered all over the room—on the sofa, on beanbag chairs, and on the floor.

In the corner of the room, beside Ms. Miller's

desk, an easel held a thick stack of charts. Ms. Miller opened to the first chart, a diagram of the female reproductive system, and began explaining how each of the organs contributed to making a baby. Blair shouted out that her mother had had her tubes tied over the summer, and Ms. Miller said that that was interesting and that, yes, health class was an informal setting and we should feel free to share our thoughts but that we should still raise our hands first. Then Anna Miles raised her hand and observed that all the organs together—the uterus, the fallopian tubes, and the ovaries—looked like the head of a ram. Ms. Miller said she hadn't thought of it that way.

No one said anything when Ms. Miller discussed the chart showing the male reproductive system, until Blair said "vas deferens" in this heavy German accent and we all cracked up.

Next, Ms. Miller flipped to a chart that explained heterosexual reproduction at the cell level. Ms. Miller talked about how the male cell and the female cell meet and combine. Ms. Miller had five kids, so we had to assume she knew what she was talking about.

I'd heard people complain about when their mother or father sat them down to give them The Talk, but as far back as I could remember, I'd always known where babies came from, at least at some level. Dad never told me stories about storks or said you had to be married to have a baby or anything like that.

About halfway through health class, there was a knocking at the door. Ms. Miller opened it, and we all saw Sam standing there, breathing hard, like he'd just done twenty push-ups. "Mr. Pohler wants to know if you're done using the charts," he said.

"Sure," Ms. Miller said, pulling the set of charts off the easel and handing it to him. Sam looked at me, then blushed and turned away, closing the door behind him. Blair giggled and whispered something to Sarah.

"Blair, what's funny?" Ms. Miller asked.

"Nothing," Blair said.

"There are no secrets in health class," Ms. Miller said.

"Sam has a mad crush on Genie. It's so obvious."

"That may or may not be true," Ms. Miller said. "But it's none of our business. Respect each other. Give each other room to grow."

Ms. Miller had us all turn to face the whiteboard so she could start to talk about some of the general changes that accompanied "that special time of life we know as puberty." Some of us were already experiencing puberty, if wearing bras was any indication, which I knew it was. Rebecca, Blair, and Macy wore them. Sarah had come back from winter break with one, even though I wasn't sure she needed one yet.

Was it time for me to get a bra too? I decided I'd talk to Dad about it when I got home that day. I could talk to Gran, but she would probably suggest that I wear some old-fashioned undershirt or something.

Toward the end of class, Ms. Miller asked if we had questions. Anna Miles raised her hand: "What is PNS?"

"Do you mean PMS?" said Ms. Miller gently.

"No, I think it's PNS," said Anna Miles. "Prenestral syndrome or something?"

"Prenestral syndrome?" Blair shouted out from the other side of the room. "Prenestral? That's not even a *word*!"

Anna Miles teared up.

"Blair," said Ms. Miller sharply. "This is an open and confidential forum. We do not critique each other's questions and comments." She turned to Anna Miles. "That's an excellent question, Anna Miles. PMS stands for premenstrual syndrome." She wrote the letters on the board. "Pre. Menstrual. Syndrome. Some women experience a few days of symptoms— mood swings, bloating, and other types of discomfort—before the onset of their period every month. We'll talk more about that tomorrow."

As I walked down the hall after health class, Blair caught up to me: "I wasn't kidding about Sam. He is totally into you, in his sweaty, husky-department kind of way."

I didn't respond.

"How's what's-his-name in your neighborhood?" Blair asked. "Your crush."

"Fine," I said, ducking into the bathroom to avoid further interrogation.

In carpool that afternoon, Sarah got a text message from some guy named Marshall. "Oh my God!" she whispered.

I looked over her shoulder. "Who's Marshall?" I whispered. Nora was at a friend's house or she would have been right in the middle of this.

"He's one of these guys Blair and I met over winter break. Their room was down the hall from ours."

"You guys had your own room?"

"Yeah, her parents stayed in one room, and we stayed next door."

I looked out the window at the leaf-less trees, whose dark, plain branches stood out against the white winter sky.

"Are you gonna text him back?"

"Maybe. I'm gonna forward it to Blair."

Within a minute I heard the phone buzzing again. Blair, on the job.

-∞)(∞-

After school, I wrote a new post.

The Class

Everyone in fifth grade knows what you mean when you say "the class" using that certain tone of voice. You're not talking about the fifth grade in general, or the dog obedience class you went to the night before, or the next day's history class. You're talking about sex ed.

I admit, the class is kind of embarrassing, but we're all going to be experiencing big changes in the next few years, so we might as well know what to expect, right?

Wish #11: That everyone feels free to ask questions in The Class, without having to worry about being teased.

That night, Ian came home with his report card. He'd gotten two Ds, worse grades than usual. Gran and Dad sat him down at the kitchen table and asked me to go to my room. I put on my radio, took out a blank piece of paper, and started drawing this huge clock that hung in the back of the school auditorium. Everyone called it the Shipley Clock, because the Shipley family gave it to the school a long time ago. Whenever we practiced for plays, the teachers would tell us to talk loudly enough that the clock could hear us.

I kept having to redo the clock to get it right. It was hard to make a perfect circle, and the rays of the sun on the outside of the clock had ridges that were tricky to draw.

The voices got louder downstairs, so I decided to save my bra discussion with Dad for another day.

No one commented on my blog post about The Class, which was kind of surprising, but when I got to my locker the next day, Blair slid up beside me. "Nice blog post. Uh, I wonder who that 'wish' of yours was directed at?" She put a finger to her chin and screwed her face up into a question mark.

"I was speaking to everyone in fifth grade, Blair."

"Baloney," she said.

For the second day's health class, Ms. Miller had brought in all kinds of products—birth control, feminine hygiene, et cetera. She said she was trying to demystify things for us, but Bethany thought she had said "demistify" and wanted to know what the mist was and why she wasn't showing *that* to us, and I held my breath and waited for Blair to pounce, but she didn't. Ms. Miller spelled the word on the board and told us that it meant to take the mystery out of something. Then she put a tampon into a small glass of water to demonstrate how it absorbed liquid. Did she really need to do that? We would have taken her word for it.

Near the end of class, Ms. Miller handed out small pieces of paper and asked us each to write down at least one additional question without writing our names on the papers. Then we put all the papers into a shoe box.

She sat down at her desk and pulled out the first white slip.

"I can has cheezburger!" she read.

Everybody, even Ms. Miller, laughed really loudly.

CHAPTER 16

The Rapids

not long after The Class had ended, Uncle Mike called our house to propose a trip. His friend had opened a new hotel near Rehoboth Beach, Delaware, the beach town where we went every summer. The hotel, called the Rapids, was part of a chain known for having huge indoor waterslides. Uncle Mike wanted to take Ian and me there for the weekend. I was so excited! Ian was grounded until his grades improved, but Dad and Gran made an exception for this trip.

I needed a new swimsuit, so Dad drove me to Emporia, where I found a really cute two-piece: a lemon-colored bikini top and shorts with lime-colored polka dots. On the way to the checkout, we picked up a travel-sized toothpaste and a new lip balm.

As we stood in the checkout line, debating which would be better, BananaMelon or PomeGrape gum, I suddenly remembered it: the bra! I asked Dad if we could look for one.

"Sure," he said, "we could do that. Unless you'd rather wait and do it with Gran?"

"I'd rather just look now," I said, picturing the floppy undershirt Gran might recommend.

"Sounds good," he said. We walked to the very back part of the store, to a section labeled "Intimates."

The saleslady in Intimates looked at my chest, grabbed five or six bras off a rack, and pointed me to a fitting room. She stood outside while I put each bra on, then came into the room to tug at the straps and check the fit. I wondered if I should start wearing deodorant. Would I even know if I smelled? How could you smell yourself if you were always with yourself? The saleslady was about as old as Gran but shorter and much wider, like an egg. Her perfume reminded me of the pink petals that dropped from our neighbor's tree every spring.

The fitting room had mirrors on three sides, and from where I was standing I could see a whole line of us, the saleslady and me, receding into increasingly distant sections of mirror. Smaller and smaller figures adjusting smaller and smaller bras.

A couple of the bras felt silky, like an old T-shirt. Others felt stiff, like something Gran probably wore when she was younger.

In the end, I decided to get two of the silky ones— one white, one light pink. The saleslady asked if I wanted to wear one out of the store, but I didn't. We added the bras to the basket, where they lay atop the lemon-lime polka-dot two-piece and the miniature toiletries.

Before we checked out, I asked for one more thing: deodorant. Dad said he wasn't sure I needed deodorant, but if I wanted to get it, that was fine with him. We returned to the Health and Beauty section, where I picked up a friendly looking blue cylinder of something called TweenStic.

I thought about asking to get "feminine hygiene"

products too, but they didn't seem necessary yet. No one I knew had actually gotten her period, not even the girls who already wore bras.

If puberty were a game, I would have advanced two rounds today. Bras and deodorant? Check, check.

~∞)) ((∞~

Uncle Mike came by in his truck at five o'clock on Friday afternoon. By eight o'clock we were pulling into the hotel parking lot. We were all so excited, we just tossed our bags into the room, threw on our bathing suits, and ran straight to the waterslides, which were open until nine thirty. We hadn't even eaten any dinner, only chips and sodas in the truck, but we didn't care.

The waterslides were amazing, full of drops and twists and turns. The water rushed you through the channels, and sometimes as you careened around a curve, it felt as if you weren't even breathing. The whole space roared with the sound of the motors.

Ian found another guy his age to hang out with.

The guy had really shaggy brown hair that covered his eyes just as Ian's did.

Uncle Mike and I stuck together. He almost lost his shorts a few times when he landed at the bottom of a waterslide, which was funny, but my two-piece stayed on really well.

We ordered pizza when we got back to the room, but I fell asleep watching *The Phantom Menace* before the pizza had even arrived. It was the best night!

⌒⊙) (⊙⌒

The next morning, we slept until eight o'clock, then drove to downtown Rehoboth. I'd never seen the town in winter before. The stores were quiet and the streets empty, as if the cold weather was a giant wave that had washed in and swept summer out to sea.

We headed for Blueberry Morning, our favorite Rehoboth breakfast place. Even in the middle of winter, when the rest of the town was a wasteland, Blueberry Morning was still crowded. That's how good the food was.

Blueberry Morning was famous for its pancakes, which were as big as Frisbees. It took at least two glasses of milk to wash them down. No one except Uncle Mike could finish a whole plateful. We all ordered them, of course.

While we were waiting for our pancakes, I remembered that we would be writing restaurant reviews in English next month. I decided that I would definitely write about Blueberry Morning. You know how tables at restaurants sometimes smelled terrible, as if the rag used to wipe them wasn't really clean? Tables at Blueberry Morning never smelled like that.

We spent a lot more time on the waterslides on Saturday afternoon and Sunday morning, then checked out of the Rapids at noon and started driving back to Baltimore.

On the way, Uncle Mike told us about some of his latest get-rich-quick product ideas. One was the

Rubber Baby
Booger Puller

Rubber Baby Booger Puller, a sort of rubbery tweezers thing that would help deal with "a chronic problem of the baby years," he said. At a stoplight in George-town, Delaware, he drew us a picture.

If nothing else, "Rubber Baby Booger Puller" made a fun tongue twister. I tried to say it ten times. Can you make money off a tongue twister? If so, Uncle Mike will try.

His second idea was the No-Foul Towel, a towel with two different sides of two different colors, one labeled "top" and one labeled "bottom." The No-Foul Towel, Uncle Mike said, would eliminate the unpleas-ant situation where you dry your face with part of a towel you'd also used to dry your butt. Uncle Mike was thinking of marketing the idea to colleges with two school colors, using one school color on one side and the second school color on the other side. Ian asked how you would decide which color to make the butt-side color, and Uncle Mike raised his eyebrows and said he'd have to think about that.

Finally, there was Uncle Mike's idea number three: Halloweenies, orange-and-black hot dogs printed with spiders and witches and broomsticks and specially served at Halloween. He said he'd heard the word *Halloweenies* used before, but he wanted to be the first—that he knew of, anyway—to develop Halloweenies into a nationwide product.

As we drove down the highway, I watched the wires pass—*zwoop, zwoop, zwoop*—along the side of the road, to and from infinity, and pretty soon I dropped off to sleep.

Uncle Mike

I spent the weekend with my Uncle Mike, who's a businessperson but really wants to be an inventor. He has a million and one product ideas and a whole ocean of wishes, hopes, and dreams. New ideas just keep coming to him. If one idea doesn't work out, Uncle Mike doesn't get depressed; he just waits for the next.

Wish #12: That there's a little Uncle Mike inside all of us.

....

JACK   Is your Uncle Mike behind those upside-down ketchup bottles? Because. Those. Are. AWESOME.

....

WALKER   There's a little Uncle Mike inside of me, but my doctor said I had to have it removed. Now I don't know what to do!

CHAPTER 17

Pip

 few days after I returned from the Rapids, Gran handed me a sparkly lilac-colored envelope with my name written on the front. "What is it?" I asked.

"I don't know," she said. "It came yesterday. I forgot to give it to you." She left the room and went upstairs.

The envelope opened at one end, down past the stamp. Inside, there was an invitation to a party at Blair's.

What was Pip? What was a preview party?

⚭))(⚭

When I got to school, everyone was talking about the party. It turned out that Blair and her mom were the new local representatives for Pip, a British makeup company. "My au pair uses *all* the Pip stuff," Blair said, pulling a small booklet out of her desk and handing it to Rebecca. "Here's the catalog. It's the coolest. See, I'm wearing their LipKisserz." She puckered her shiny mouth.

"I've never even heard of it," Rebecca said, flipping pages.

"You can only get it through Pip parties," Blair said. "Sare is going to be the model. My mom's gonna do a makeover on her. Mom will do other people too if there's time."

"Can you make me look pretty?" Jack said, pushing his lips out like a fish.

"You aren't invited, fish face!" Blair said, shoving him sideways.

"We can try some of the products at the party, right?" Bethany asked.

"Right. And everyone who comes gets a Pip beauty-rest mask, a pack of Pip gum, and some other stuff," Blair said. She blew a big pink Pip bubble.

"Blair," Mr. Sayler said, staring hard at her from

behind his desk. Blair wrapped her gum inside a tissue, then sauntered over to the trash can in the corner of the classroom.

The day was cold and rainy, so recess was in the gym. I played four-square for a while, then sat down on the floor with Sarah and Blair, who were looking at the Pip catalog. Even though Sarah and I still did carpool together, I missed her. We hadn't had a sleepover in a long time.

"Are you coming to the preview party?" Sarah asked me.

"Maybe," I said. "Can I look at the catalog?"

"Sure," she said.

I flipped through the pages. The catalog was small, more like a Junie B. Jones book than an issue of *Tween Life*. All the models looked like teenagers.

"You should have your mom do a makeover on Genie instead of me," Sarah said.

Blair shook her head.

Sarah persisted. "Then she could write about it on her blog, and you'd get even more orders!"

Blair paused and considered it for a second. "Nah."

I thought about the transitive property of friendship again, the one I'd wondered about at the beginning of the year. I was pretty sure that this property didn't exist. Nearly half a year later, A and C were still barely more than acquaintances.

CHAPTER 18

Spirit Day of Service

t HCD's annual Day of Service, you could make scarves for veterans or valentines for the elderly. You could make sandwiches for a soup kitchen, paint a mural on the walls of a local school, or clear trash off the banks of a city stream. Sarah and I had both signed up for the sandwich-making activity. Unfortunately, so had Blair.

At the last minute, after the Baltimore Ravens made the play-offs, Mr. Graham decided to combine the Day of Service with a spirit day to make a Spirit Day of Service. So while you were doing all this serving, you'd be wearing team colors or actual Ravens gear.

Here's everything I knew about football:

1. Watching it made Dad yell like he never did at any other time.

2. People often explained the size of big things in terms of football fields (as in, *All the refrigerators thrown out in the United States last year would fill twenty football fields*).

3. Somehow, it took about three hours to play four fifteen-minute quarters.

4. The Ravens' colors were purple and black.

On the morning of the Spirit Day of Service, I put on a purple T-shirt, a pair of black leggings, and a short black skirt. Ian let me borrow his Ravens skull-cap. When I got to the cafeteria, Sophie was there, wearing a black shirt, jeans, and purple Converse sneakers.

"Cool, are you doing the sandwich thing?" she asked.

"Yeah," I said. "I like your sneakers."

"Thanks!" she said.

Blair showed up next. She was wearing purple lip-stick, glittery maroon eye shadow, a cropped Ravens jersey, and a pair of sweatpants with "Ravens" written across the butt. Her white-blond ponytail jutted out from one side of her head like a handlebar.

"Where's Sare?" she asked.

"I don't know," I said.

Ms. Durst walked in from the kitchen carrying huge containers of soy butter and grape jelly. She wore a Ravens jersey that hung down almost to her knees.

We followed her back into the kitchen, which looked like a place made for giants, not regular humans. Everything was enormous—from the cans of baked beans to the metal pots.

Ms. Durst gestured to the shelves where the bread loaves were stacked. Blair and I both grabbed some. Sophie picked up another tub of soy butter. "Where's everyone else?" Blair asked.

"Well, you three girls, plus Sarah White, were the only ones who signed up for this activity, and, as it turns out, Sarah is sick today. So it's just us! Hope you're ready to work!"

"Don't we need more people?" Blair asked.

"We'll be fine," Ms. Durst said. "Have a little faith!"

Thank God for Sophie, I thought. I might not survive an entire day alone with Blair.

We set up a production line. I spread the soy butter on one slice of bread and then passed the slice to Sophie. Sophie spread the jelly on a second slice of bread, then put that slice on top of my soy butter slice. Blair cut the sandwich in two, then wrapped it in aluminum foil. Finally, Ms. Durst put the sandwich in a big plastic tub with a lid that was marked "Pete's Kitchen."

About fifty sandwiches in, Ms. Durst got a phone call. "I've got to run over to the middle school, ladies. Keep going, and I'll be back ASAP."

Blair wiped the back of her hand against her cheek. "When are we getting out of here?"

"When we're done, I guess," Sophie said.

Blair sighed. "I wish I'd signed up for something

where I didn't have to be in the stupid cafeteria with *nobody* all morning." She walked to the back of the room, pulled out her phone, and started texting.

Sophie and I kept spreading. Soon, we had two towers of sandwiches that needed to be halved and wrapped.

"Are you coming back?" I said to Blair.

"In a minute."

Just then, Drew and Jack cut through the front of the cafeteria.

"Guys!" Blair said, suddenly sounding breathless. "What's up? Where are you going?"

"That stream-cleanup thing," Jack said.

"I'm coming with you," Blair said.

"Blair?" I said, pointing to the sandwich pile.

There was no stopping her, even if we wanted to. She was gone.

"I mean, I don't know Blair very well," Sophie said, "and I know she's a good friend of yours, but she seems totally boy *crazy*. Or even boy *insane*."

"I *know!*" Hearing Sophie say what I was thinking was such a relief. "And she's not really that good a friend of mine. Mostly she's a friend of Sarah's."

"I'm going to her party," Sophie said, "but I probably can't buy anything. I'm not allowed to wear makeup. Are you?"

"I don't know." Was I? Dad and I had never talked about it.

Ms. Durst came back into the room. "Where's Blair?" she asked.

"She went off with the stream-cleanup group," I said.

"The sandwiches weren't entertaining enough?"

"I guess not," Sophie said.

Spirit Day of Service

It was pretty cool seeing everyone doing their service projects at school in Ravens colors today. I was in the group making soy butter and jelly (grape—Ravens purple!) sandwiches. Our group started small and got smaller, but we still made hundreds of sandwiches, enough to feed a bunch of hungry people. What were you guys doing?

Wish #13: That today's HCD projects end up helping a lot of people.

....

(SOPHIE) It was so much fun making sandwiches with you!

....

(JOSH) My group went to Hopkins Hospital to work with some of the kids there. It was really awesome.

....

(BETHANY) My group went to the senior citizens' home where my grandparents live!!! That was awesome too.

....

(ANNA MILES) Cool, Bethany! I saw some really sick pets at the SPCA. One of them barely had any fur left. I hope they get better!

CHAPTER 19

Fortune Cookie

not long after the Spirit Day of Service, Macy invited Anna Miles, Sophie, and me to a restaurant with her family to celebrate her eleventh birthday. Dad and I gave Sophie a ride.

When Dad dropped us off, Macy, her parents, and her older brother, Duaine, were already seated in the back of the restaurant with Anna Miles. Macy's mother, Mrs. Buxton, stood up and waved us over.

"Hello, ladies," Mr. Buxton said, standing up at his chair.

"Look!" Macy said as we sat down. She pulled back her hair and pointed to her ears.

"Oh my gosh!" Sophie said.

"Mom took me to the doctor this afternoon to have it done!"

"Did it hurt?" I asked.

"Not really," Macy said. "Mom didn't have to hold my hand or anything." With her earrings, Macy looked older now, more like her mother. Her new silver stud earrings shone brightly against her dark brown skin.

Mr. and Mrs. Buxton had both been part of the previous year's HCD Career Day panel. He was a bio-medical engineer who worked on gene therapy, and she ran a store that specialized in finding just the right pair of jeans for every woman. ("He does gene therapy; I do jean therapy," Mrs. Buxton liked to say.) This explained why Macy always had brands of jeans I'd never heard of, with unfamiliar back-pocket designs.

"Macy, your ears are a little red. Are they getting infected?" Mrs. Buxton said.

"They're fine, Mom," Duaine said, looking up from his phone.

"You would know? You're a doctor now?" said Mrs. Buxton.

"They're fine, Mom," Macy said.

"You'll tell me if they start hurting a lot?" Mrs. Buxton said, her eyebrows pushing together.

"Yes, Mom."

"How about you, Genie? When are you getting your ears pierced?" Mrs. Buxton asked.

"When I'm twelve."

"Who's the holdout, your dad or your mom?" She quickly correctly herself. "I mean, your grandmother."

"My dad, I guess," I said.

"That's all right. You all grow up fast enough—no need to rush things. Speaking of which, are you going to this Blair person's makeup party on Saturday?"

Sophie, Anna Miles, and I said we probably were.

"I'd like to know why eleven-year-old girls need to have a makeup party," Mrs. Buxton said.

"It's just for fun, Mom," Macy said. "Nothing serious."

"It's not a make-*out* party, Mom," Duaine said.

"Very funny, Duaine. I just haven't decided," Mrs. Buxton said. She reapplied her lipstick, then pressed a tissue against her mouth.

The waitress came for our orders. I hadn't even had time to look at the menu. "Can we get sodas, Mom?" Macy asked. "Just this one time?"

"Mom, it's not like they're asking for beer," Duaine said.

"Yes, you all may have sodas," Mrs. Buxton said.

"Thanks, Mom," Macy said.

Mr. Buxton looked up from the menu. "I'd like to order for the table. Family style. That okay with everyone?"

It was.

∞◯) (◯∞

I drank two whole glasses of soda while we waited for the food, so pretty soon I had to excuse myself. Mr. Buxton pointed to the other side of the restaurant. "Just head toward that cat," he said. I followed his finger and saw a white ceramic cat on a high shelf. I'd seen cats like that in restaurants before and always liked them.

Then I saw something far less expected. I saw Sarah in a glittery one-shoulder top, sitting at a table with Blair, Rebecca, and Blair's mother. Sarah was laughing.

"Genie!" Rebecca called out.

"Hi," I said, walking toward their table, the caps of my knees shaking wildly. Blair whispered something to Sarah, who shifted inside her glittery shirt. I noticed that Blair, Sarah, and Rebecca were all wearing the same cherry-colored lip gloss. From Pip, I assumed.

"Who's this?" Blair's mom said.

"I'm Genie."

"Miss Blogtacular," Blair said.

"Miss what?" asked Blair's mom.

"Nothing," said Blair.

"Are you seeing *Vampyr City* tonight too?" her mother said.

"I'm not allowed to see R-rated movies," I said.

"That's why we didn't invite you," Rebecca said. "We didn't want you to feel bad."

"You've got good parents, little one," Blair's mom said, laughing. She had a southern accent that made everything she said sound fleshy and tart, like an unripe peach.

I looked down at all the food on their table—plates of noodles, egg rolls, and dumplings. "We are totally abandoning our diets—just for tonight, right, Sare?" Blair said.

"Yeah," Sarah said. She wouldn't look at me.

"I need to get back," I said. I was glad that the tablecloth concealed my shaking kneecaps, and even more glad that I had a table of friends to return to.

"Bye, little one!" Blair said.

Little one? I thought to myself as I finished the walk to the bathroom. *As if!*

Back at the table, I didn't mention seeing the others. I didn't want to ruin the Szechuan string beans, the steamed pork buns, the chicken with broccoli, or the unidentified noodle thing. Macy, Anna Miles, and Sophie wouldn't have felt bad for themselves—they weren't that close to Sarah, Rebecca, and Blair, anyway—but they would have felt awkward for me. Sarah was still supposed to be my best friend.

At the end of dinner, the server brought a plate of fortune cookies, and we ate them instead of birthday cake, which probably came as some relief to Mrs. Buxton, after all that soda.

Leavening

I got a fortune cookie tonight that made me think of the Wishes, Hopes, and Dreams theme of our blog. It said, "Hope puts a bounce in the heart." Did they mean "a bounce in the step"? Or "a bounce in your step"? Anyway, I know what they meant. Hope is helpful. It's a kind of leavening, like the yeast in the bread my dad and I make sometimes. (Speaking of bread, my dad says girls our age shouldn't put themselves on diets.)

Wish #14: That hope puts a bounce in your heart.

....

BLAIR   Vampyr Richard puts a bounce in my heart. Oh, and also? *My* dad says guys don't make passes at girls with fat . . . !

....

REBECCA   Blair Annabelle Lea, watch your mouth!

That night, Sarah sent me an e-mail with the subject line "Sorry!!!" She said she hadn't told me about movie night with Blair and Rebecca because she hadn't wanted me to feel bad that I couldn't go. I e-mailed back and told her it was okay.

Then she e-mailed back to say she was so full from all the food at dinner and had totally messed up on her diet, and I e-mailed back to say she looked completely fine and was the last person who needed to be on a diet. Then she e-mailed back to say thanks.

The next morning, Blair saw Sarah and me talking at the lockers. "Little one!" Blair called out. "That's your new nickname!" Then she skipped over to Hassan and Drew, and Drew pulled Blair's white-blond ponytail, and Blair screeched with pain but mostly delight.

In English class that day, Mrs. Hanson started a unit on persuasive writing. She began by talking about how persuasive writing is writing with a clear purpose: to convince readers to come around to the writer's point of view about something, whether it's the beauty of a travel destination or a truth about human existence.

As an example, she threw out the topic of Junk Food Lunch, the subject of my first blog post. "Now, Genie's blog post wished for something without truly making the case for it. And as you all noticed, Junk Food Lunch didn't return. Maybe Genie needed to do more than just wish. Maybe she needed to explain the wish, to give *reasons why* the wish should be granted."

Mrs. Hanson picked up a piece of chalk and asked us to brainstorm reasons why Junk Food Lunch was actually a good thing. Within ten minutes, there were nineteen or twenty reasons listed, some better than others.

"Check it out, Genie," Mrs. Hanson said. "There are a few great points here."

I nodded.

"We'll talk more about persuasive writing tomorrow," Mrs. Hanson said, lifting a stack of papers off her desk. "But right now I want to switch gears." She passed out copies of a poem by Emily Dickinson. "Who can tell me who Emily Dickinson was?" she asked.

Walker raised his hand: "A reclusive nineteenth-century American poet who liked to use dashes a lot." Walker's mom was an English professor at Johns Hopkins.

"Good," Mrs. Hanson said. "Did anybody read Genie's blog post last night? First of all, she's totally right, not one of you girls needs to be on a diet. But I'm thinking about the fortune cookie part. It made me think of this Emily Dickinson poem." She crossed her legs and put her pencil behind her ear. "Genie, would you like to read it?"

The poem, like the fortune from the cookie, was about hope. My favorite part was the beginning: "Hope is the thing with feathers / that perches in the soul."

"Now we have three different metaphors for hope. Genie's fortune cookie said that hope was something that put a bounce in your heart. Genie offered her own alternative, saying that hope was a kind of leavening. Now, what metaphor does Emily Dickinson use for hope?"

"A bird," Sophie said. "A bird that's always with you."

"Precisely," Mrs. Hanson said.

"Weird fact," said Sophie. "My name is an anagram for 'hope is.' That's one of the reasons my parents named me Sophie."

"How neat!" Mrs. Hanson said. She walked back behind her desk and started shifting papers around. "Okay, we're out of time. Fly, my little birds, fly!"

That night, I wrote a new Junk Food Lunch post—a more persuasive one, I hoped.

JFL, Take 2

The parents' association wants the best for us, I know, but we fifth graders still think they shouldn't have gotten rid of Junk Food Lunch. Here are just a few of the many reasons why Junk Food Lunch deserves to return.

❶ **Everything in moderation.** My grandmother always says this. If you eat a little bit of something, you won't be tempted to eat a ton of it later.

❷ **A's are great grades.** Let's say we are in school for 20 days out of a month. If 1 of those 20 days involves a Junk Food Lunch, that's only 5 percent of the month. That means that 95 percent of the lunches are really healthy (turkey sandwiches, raw vegetables, etc.). A 95 is an A, and an A is a really great grade!

3 **We work hard.** Things like Junk Food Lunch pay off for HCD in the long run. Sure, it's not the healthiest food. Everyone knows that. But it's a good reward for all the hard work we do every day. It makes us work even harder, the same way an extra 10 minutes of recess does.

4 **It's not all junk, anyway.** Pizza has tomato sauce, which is good for you. French fries involve potatoes, which are real things that grow in the ground.

Wish #15: That Junk Food Lunch will come back, for all the reasons noted above!

REBECCA I will pay for it myself. Really!

SOPHIE Good job, Genie!

CHAPTER 20

Cul-de-Sac

J had a lot of hope for the second Junk Food Lunch post. Mrs. Hanson had told me it was far more persuasive than the first one I'd written.

Blair's Pip party was scheduled to run from two o'clock to four o'clock on Saturday, so Dad and I got into his car at one thirty. I was wearing a pair of jeans and a lime-green T-shirt. In my hand I held my wallet and a map I'd printed off the Internet.

"Blair's the new girl this year, right?"

"Right. The one who went to camp with Sarah."

"What's the wallet for?"

"They're selling makeup at the party."

"Makeup?"

"Yeah."

"What do you need with makeup? You're ten."

"I know. I probably won't buy anything."

"No eye makeup, okay? Lip stuff maybe. That's it."

We got on the expressway and drove about fifteen minutes north, past farms with horses. Eventually we pulled into a development with a big stone sign marked Paradise Mews, then turned onto a street called Adam Road. Blair's house was at the end of Adam Road. A *cul-de-sac*, Dad called it.

I jumped out of the car, leaving my coat behind. "Are you going to be warm enough?" Dad asked.

"I'm fine," I said.

"See you in a bit. Call my cell phone if you need me."

I could see my face reflected in the side windows of the car, my skin pale and my eyes dark and plain.

An older girl I didn't recognize opened the front door of Blair's house. "Hi, I'm Marta," she said in a thick Spanish accent. "I'm the au pair."

"Hi," I said.

"Everyone's in the sunroom," she said, pointing to her left.

I followed the noise into a bright, crowded room where Mrs. Lea, Blair, and Sarah were passing out cups of punch.

Sarah brought me a cup. "It's diet punch," she said.

Diet punch? I'd never heard of that before.

Macy ran over to me. "Mom let me come to the party!"

"Cool!" I said. We sat down next to each other, and I sipped the pink bubbly punch with the weird after-taste. A banner strung up on one side of the room screamed "PIPtastic!"

"Get this, Genie," Macy said. "Somebody snapped my bra yesterday when I was looking for books in the library."

"Ow," I said. "Who was it?"

"I don't know. I whipped my head around, but whoever it was had run into another aisle. It's happened to at least five people since that first time with Rebecca," she said.

"Wow," I said, thinking about the bras in my drawer at home. I'd started wearing the deodorant, but I still hadn't worn the bras outside the house.

After a final few girls came into the room, Mrs. Lea asked everyone to quiet down. "Thanks for coming, y'all. It's really exciting to have y'all here and to be able to introduce y'all to this really cool makeup. Pip products are all-natural and good for your skin, and Pip supports impoverished people around the world. As a special deal for y'all, y'all get an extra ten percent off any orders you place today.

"Now, I know a lot of y'all are new to makeup, so we're going to walk y'all through each product and let you know what it's for. Our volunteer model for the day is the lovely Sarah White." Sarah smiled. She was wearing a headband that pulled her hair back from her face.

"I'm gonna show y'all how Pip products can make an already-pretty girl like Sarah even prettier. Y'all don't need much. Just a light, light touch.

"We'll start with some of our tinted moisturizer. It's got a good SPF so you don't get sun damage like I've got." She squeezed some of the moisturizer onto her fingers and dabbed it on different parts of Sarah's face, then began rubbing it in.

"You want to get a good match on the color so it blends into your skin. Sarah is wearing the lightest color, which is called Fair. There's also Medium and Dark. If you're between shades, you can always mix them. And if you've got a pimple or something, you can always put a little of the Pip concealer on first, for more coverage."

"What if I want to look tan?" Bethany asked. "Can I use a darker color?"

"Not unless you want to look like an idiot," Blair said.

"I wouldn't put it that way," Mrs. Lea said. "But Blair is correct. Stick with a natural shade and blend, blend, blend. You don't want any lines where the color ends."

Mrs. Lea moved on to blush (what Gran would call rouge), then eye shadow, eyeliner, and mascara. By the time she was done, Sarah looked like someone out of *Tween Life*.

"What do y'all think?" asked Mrs. Lea.

"I think she looks awesome!" Bethany said.

"Does anyone else want a turn?"

Bethany jumped out of her chair.

"Come on up, darlin'."

Mrs. Lea worked on Bethany for a while, explaining as she went. Then Blair said, "Okay, you guys, I'm going to pass around catalogs with order forms!" She handed a stack to Sarah, who took one and passed the rest to Anna Miles.

"Here are some pens," Blair added. "Also, if anyone wants to host a Pip party, let me know! If you host a party for us, you get a hundred-and-fifty-dollar Pip gift card!"

Everyone grabbed catalogs and started flipping through. "Y'all let me know if you have questions!" Mrs. Lea said. "And if you think of something you want later, call us or go to our Web page at the Pip site. The Web address is on the front of the catalog."

I had only ten dollars in my wallet, and almost everything in the catalog cost at least seven dollars.

"What are you ordering?" Macy asked.

"Probably just a lip gloss," I said.

"I don't think I'm allowed to get anything," Anna Miles said.

"Me neither," Macy said.

Sophie came over and sat with us. "Are you guys getting something?"

"Maybe just one thing," I said.

"When you're done with your order forms, just bring them up to me," Blair called out. "Or give them to Marta. Make sure you write down your credit card numbers."

Credit card numbers?

"Can we pay cash?" Sophie asked. I was wondering the same thing.

Blair laughed. "No! This isn't, like, a *grocery* store!"

Sophie and I glanced at each other. It looked as if we weren't going to be ordering any Piptastic products today.

Mrs. Lea finished Bethany's makeover. She looked fine, but not as pretty as Sarah did. Then again, Sarah was prettier than Bethany to begin with. It was just a fact, and no amount of makeup would change that.

Soon it was time to go. "Tell all your friends!" Blair said. "The ones from outside HCD. We're going to have more parties soon."

"Thanks for the orders, y'all," Mrs. Lea said. "And don't forget your Pip swag bags."

Pip bags stood like soldiers on a circular glass table in the entrance hall under a big crystal chandelier. I picked one up by the twisted paper handle.

"Do you need a ride home?" I asked Sarah.

"No, I'm staying here tonight," Sarah said.

"Have fun," I said.

Dad's car idled in the cul-de-sac. I put my Pip bag in the backseat, next to the rolls of canvas and other art supplies that Dad had picked up.

"How was it?" he asked.

"Fine," I said. "Kind of weird. Can we get ice cream on the way home? There was hardly anything to eat."

"Sure," he said, curling my hair back behind my

ear. "Thank God you didn't come out looking like Zsa Zsa Gabor."

"Who?"

"Oh, no one."

I looked in the rearview mirror. My skin was just as pale and my eyes just as plain and dark as they had been when I walked into the party, but that was okay with me.

CHAPTER 21

Wizards and Eagles

ne Sunday, Gran and I were in the kitchen, preparing bread for stuffing. I asked Gran why we were having turkey when it wasn't Thanksgiving, and she said that any day was a good day to be thankful, and that anyway we all liked turkey. Gran always liked to break the bread for stuffing by hand rather than chopping it in a food processor. She said it made the stuffing taste better.

"Genie," Gran said, twirling the wedding ring she still wore. "How do you think Ian is doing right now?"

"He seems quiet. Or bored. More than usual."

"Eighth-grade boys are complicated characters. I remember when your father was this age, he would barely speak to your grandfather and me, but then one of his little girlfriends would call on the phone, and he'd perk right up. Boys his age really want to be independent, and they get frustrated by their families a lot. We shouldn't take it personally. Look how well your father and I get on now."

Gran went to the sink to rinse the crumbs from her hands. I kept breaking bread, even though the mound of bread crumbs had nearly reached the top of the bowl.

There was a very old radio on a shelf in our kitchen. It no longer worked, but we still liked it. Gran's own grandmother had once written down a recipe for brownies while listening to this radio. We called them Static Brownies, since my great-great-grandmother had had to listen through the static to get the recipe right.

Gran sat down next to me, wiping her hands on a dish towel. "I'm thinking of suggesting that Ian get a part-time job. He's young for a real job, but he might be able to find something. Work might take his mind off any concerns he has and make him feel a bit more self-sufficient. If nothing else, it would give him some walking-around money, which he'll need as he gets older." She paused. "Allowance is good, but money you've earned yourself is even better. It gives you pride."

"Maybe Margo could help," I said. "Remember how at Christmas she mentioned her two brothers with businesses?"

"That's a great idea," Gran said. "You're a genie *and* a wizard!" She hugged me around the shoulders. "I'll call her." Gran and Margo had struck up a kind of friendship ever since Margo had expressed interest in learning how to crochet.

I thought back to last summer, when Ian worked behind the snack counter at our pool for a couple of

hours one day, a last-minute substitute for a guy who'd broken his arm. Ian had looked completely bored, even when his friends came in to order food. How would he handle a real job?

Pocket Change

Today I was talking to my grandmother about jobs and money and kids. I guess every fifth grader probably gets allowance now, and eventually we'll have grown-up jobs, but in between we'll have little jobs that teach us some skills and put some money into our pocket. That's good. When you're getting only $5 a week, it takes forever to save for anything really big.

Even my Uncle Mike (remember him?), who's sure that one of his inventions will hit it big someday, has a regular job. He needs his pocket change too!

Wish #16: That we'll find good jobs when we're ready for them!

....

BLAIR   And if you need a place to spend your pocket change, just call me for some Piptastic makeup! Or go to www.pipmakeup.com/Leaward.

BETHANY When is my ginormous order going to get here?

BLAIR Soon! Probably in a week.

After we ate turkey that night and Ian left for the movies with some friends (he wasn't grounded anymore), Dad, Margo, and Gran talked about Ian's job prospects. It turned out that one of Margo's brothers owned the Let Freedom Ring tax-preparation franchise near our house. No matter how cold it was, this place always had one or two people standing out front in patriotic costumes, waving at traffic. Margo's brother was looking for someone to work on Monday and Wednesday afternoons and would pay Ian eight dollars an hour if he wanted the job. Eight dollars! In one hour!

Ian might hate dressing in a patriotic costume, and he might not like the fact that Margo got him the

job, but I was sure that he'd like making eight dollars
an hour.

On Ian's second day at work, Mrs. White had to do an
errand before the Whites dropped me off after school.
She drove down Cold Spring Lane. As we approached
Let Freedom Ring, I scrunched down in my seat.

A person was standing out on the sidewalk in an
eagle costume, waving steadily. I knew it was Ian—I
could just tell from the way that he waved. It was the
smallest possible movement that could actually count
as a wave.

183

CHAPTER 22

Valentine's Day

The real Valentine's Day fell on a weekend, so we didn't have our official school Valentine's celebration until the following Monday. The younger kids always had parties with games and craft activities, but kids in the older grades didn't. A couple of people would give out cards and candy to everyone in the class, but most people didn't do anything. I'd completely forgotten about it until I got to the classroom and saw a Batman valentine from Sam, the patty melt/Milk Duds king, on my desk. I looked around and was relieved to see the same card on all the other desks.

As it happened, it was my first day wearing a bra to school. The Emporia bag had been sitting in my dresser drawer for weeks. I didn't know what had taken me so long.

At snack we had heart-shaped cookies that Mrs. Baumann had sent in with Rebecca. Bethany and Blair were wearing all their Pip makeup—for Valentine's Day, I guess. They looked out of place, almost like mannequins who had joined our class.

At recess, Sophie and I stood in line, waiting for a turn at four-square. I felt weird about my bra and hoped no one would try to snap it.

"I was wondering," Sophie said, "do you want to join my softball team? My dad is the coach."

"Yeah, that'd be great," I said. I still had the baseball glove that my grandfather had bought me, the one we'd used to play catch in the triangular park near our house.

"I'll get my dad to call your dad," Sophie said. "Would your dad be able to help coach?"

"Maybe," I said, imagining my dad behind first base, knobby knees sticking out from below his shorts.

On the way home in carpool, Sarah whispered, "Are you wearing a bra?"

"What?" Nora said loudly.

"Nothing," Sarah hissed back.

I nodded.

"Did anybody snap it today?"

"No, thank God," I said.

"Drew snapped mine last week at lunch. He's such a lame-o."

"Everything okay back there?" Mrs. White asked, her big round sunglasses appearing in the rearview mirror.

"Yes," Sarah and I said in unison.

"When did you get it?" Sarah asked.

"A couple of weeks ago. But I just started wearing it."

"Jack left me a valentine," Sarah whispered. "In

my locker. Plus, that guy Marshall from the ski place texted me a valentine."

"Oh my gosh!" I said.

"And Drew put a box of chocolates in Blair's desk!"

"She'll never eat them," I joked.

"What?" Nora said again.

"Nothing!" Sarah hissed.

Nora started to cry. "Sarah and Genie won't tell me what they're talking about!"

"Mom!" Sarah yelled.

"Nora, remember that Sarah and Genie have been friends a long time, and they have their own secrets, just like you and I do," Mrs. White said.

"We don't have any secrets," Nora said, pouting out the window.

When I got home, I found a crumpled-up note at the bottom of my backpack. It had just a Web site address written on it, nothing else. I figured it had gotten into my backpack by accident, but after I finished my homework, I went onto Dad's computer and typed the address into the browser. A page came up. "Hassan Says" was written at the top, and underneath were blog entries.

A lot of the entries went something like this:

Dudes, check out these videos my friend Derek posted on YouTube. They're hilarious. The ones with the ferret are the best.

But it was the first item on the page, the one posted just a few minutes earlier, that seared into my memory:

Genie Wishes didn't think The Class was so bad. Maybe it made her WISH for a bra? She's got one now—did you notice?—just in time for Valentine's Day!

··

DREW   Yeah.

··

DREW   P.S. New name for Macy: Macy BUXOM.

I sat still in the chair, my heart thumping out of my chest. This was the same Hassan I'd had English and math with for years? The one who always had neatly combed hair and freshly ironed clothes? The one I'd beaten in the class blogger election?

CHAPTER 23

Ragged Claws

henever I thought about the scrap of paper and the blog it had led me to, my heart would start thumping again and my stomach would hurt. I'd kind of lost interest in blogging. I'd even stopped looking at Eve's Reads.

But when Mr. Sayler suggested that I blog about the class graduation party, so people could start working on their costumes, I knew I didn't really have a choice.

Graduation Party

After our lower school graduation there's going to be a nighttime costume party at Sarah's house, with the theme "Under the Sea." We can swim and eat and hang out.

Wish #17: That it's a fun party.

....

SARAH Yay! Also, guys, my mother is going to hire a caterer for the party, so let me know what kind of stuff you want to eat. And what games you want to play.

....

JACK I might dress as an octopus. That way I'll have eight arms and can win pretty much any game.

....

JACK Also, Hassan is dressing as Neptune.

....

REBECCA No one better throw me into the pool! Not even the god of the sea!

....

WALKER [[[..]]] <— scuttling crab, ragged claws (T. S. Eliot)

....

WALKER P.S. Has anyone seen my hermit crab, Snakey? I brought it to school for lunch the other day—I mean, not so I could eat it for lunch, so it could HAVE lunch. And then I lost it. Rats. I mean hermit crabs. :(

The next day, Blair talked to me outside our lockers. "Why didn't you ever blog about my Pip party?"

"Why would I?"

"Because it was something involving all the girls in the class. And because it was totally fun."

"The blog theme is Wishes, Hopes, and Dreams. What does makeup have to do with that?"

Blair sighed. "A lot! Anyway, you've written about both of Sarah's parties now, the slumber party *and* the graduation party."

"That's different," I said.

"I don't think it is," Blair said. "Could you at least link to the Web page where people can order stuff?"

"You already put the link on the blog the other day, in your comment," I said.

"Geez," Blair said. She walked away, her ponytail flicking from side to side, the way cats' tails do when the cats don't get their way.

∞◯) (◯∞

In carpool later that day Sarah asked me if I would reconsider posting about the Pip products. Not about the party exactly, but about how you could order the products from Blair and about how cool they were. She said it would mean a lot to Blair.

"Sorry, I'm just not going to," I said.

"I think you're being stubborn," Sarah said, looking out the window. "Maybe even a little bit mean."

That night, I must have flipped my pillow to the cold side a thousand times before I finally fell asleep. Was I being mean, or was I just standing my ground? How would I know?

∞◯) (◯∞

I kept the piece of paper with the URL to Hassan's blog in the same drawer where I kept my bras and deodorant. Every couple of days, I went back to the blog. There was a lot of talk about video games. Movies. Music. Legos. TV. A poster named QT had started commenting on everything, even lots of the older posts. On the Valentine's Day post, the one about my bra, he'd written, "As if she even needed one—LOL. Flat as a pancake."

Then one day QT posted a "Successful Snaps" chart he'd made. Boys' names appeared in one column, and their number of successful bra snappings appeared in column 2. Drew had four, QT had five, Hassan had one. Some other boys had a few. The chart was done in orange and black, with flames around the border. It looked like something a four-year-old boy who loved Hot Wheels would design.

The next morning I was standing at a bulletin board, reading the school calendar, when a group of boys passed behind me, laughing. I felt a quick clawing at the center of my back, and then a sharp sting. I whipped my head around without shrieking or squealing, but I saw only a patch of heads, moving away. Who had done it?

That night, I talked to my dad and Uncle Mike about the bra-snapping thing. Not Hassan's blog, just the snapping. Dad said he'd never snapped a bra, but Uncle Mike said he'd had some experience in this department. I wasn't too surprised. His recommendation? Tell the girls to stop reacting. The reactions encouraged the boys, he said.

But I didn't want to write to just the girls. I was the class blogger, after all. So, on the last night before spring break, I wrote a post for everyone.

Grow Up!

We need to talk. Seriously. Remember what happened during the Christmas wrapping party? What Ms. Miller talked to us about? It's still happening, and, honestly, it's stupid and annoying. So here's what I wanted to say. *Guys:* Stop. Find a new hobby. *Girls:* Stop reacting (shrieking, etc.). It just makes the boys do it more. My Uncle Mike says so.

Wish #18: That you guys will find better things to occupy your time!

⚬◗) (◖⚬

The next morning, Drew and Blair came up behind me at my locker. "Oooh, snap!" Drew said. "You really told us off."

I could feel my face going hot and cherry-red, but I stayed where I was.

"So, just to clarify," Blair said, "how is a lecture about bra snapping more closely related to wishes, hopes, and dreams than Pip makeup is?"

Drew cracked up.

They were perfect for each other.

CHAPTER 24

Spring Break

pring break couldn't have come at a better time. I needed a break from everything: Blair, the bra snapping, and the blog.

At our school, spring break began during the second week of March. Some people would fly off with their families to beaches, ski resorts, or European cities. Often, they came back tanned. My family usually took a couple of day trips—to Washington, DC, or colonial Williamsburg—and I was more likely to come back with a souvenir visor than a tan.

I wouldn't be seeing Sarah at all this vacation, since she was jetting off to Jamaica with Blair's family. Things had gotten even more distant between Sarah and me since she'd asked me to blog about the Pip party and I'd refused. We still talked at school and in carpool, but it was different, as if an essential flavor had been left out of a recipe—sand tarts without the cinnamon or eggnog without the nutmeg.

I was happy, though, that I'd be seeing a lot of Sophie over the break, because of softball.

Our team's first game was against the Roland Park Rangers. Even though we lost, it wasn't a total disaster. I got on base twice and struck out three people in my two innings as pitcher. Dad cheered from the sidelines, served as third-base coach, and helped Sophie's father keep us organized. Gran sat off to the side in a folding chair, a bottle of water waiting in her lap for me. Between innings I ran over and took a few gulps. When it was all over, Gran patted my arm and told me how proud my grandfather would have been, which made both Gran and me tear up.

Our next game was against the Parkville Panthers. The girls were huge and hardly ever missed a pop fly. We lost, 15-0.

Our third game was against Hampden. We beat them, just barely: 6-5. Everyone leaped around when it ended. Sophie gave me a huge hug. I had to say, winning was more fun than losing.

After the Hampden game, Sophie came over to my house. The day was warm for March, and my grandfather's daffodils bloomed all over the backyard. We took out two lawn chairs from the basement, wiped the cobwebs off them, and lay out in our softball clothes to get some sun. Sophie always looked tan, but my skin was still a glowing wintry white. ("Phlegm color," Ian said.) Sophie and I talked about stuff—softball, school, and other things—while Lulu slept beside us on the warm pavement.

Lulu must have been dreaming, because occasionally she would jerk her paws and try to bark with her mouth closed. The stifled barks sounded like something you'd hear from a dolphin, not a dog. They cracked us up.

After about an hour, Gran came out and told us

that was enough, we'd gotten our vitamin D. "Remember my friend Bev," she said, looking through her silver eyeglasses at me. (Bev had had skin cancer and was fine now, but she remained Gran's go-to example when it came to the "dangers of sunbathing.")

When we came back inside, we sat down at Dad's computer.

"Are Blair and Sarah still on diets?" Sophie asked.

"I don't know. I guess so. Dieting is dumb."

"Yeah," Sophie said. "So dumb."

"They're both kind of mad at me because I haven't written about the Pip products on the class blog."

"Why would you?" she said.

"Exactly!" I said, relieved. "Hey, want to see something weird?"

"Sure," she said.

I typed in the URL, and Hassan's blog came up.

Sophie looked at it for a minute, then looked at me. "Wait a minute," she said. "Is this our Hassan?"

"Scroll through it," I said. I sat on my hands so Sophie couldn't see how badly they'd started trembling.

Sophie found the post from Valentine's Day, the one where Hassan had talked about my bra. "Oh my gosh, that's so mean!" she said.

I nodded, my eyes pooling with tears.

"I bet he's still mad that he lost the class blogger election," she said. "But what about these other guys? They have no excuse."

"A couple of weeks ago," I said, "this guy named QT got really active on the blog." I clicked on the "Successful Snaps" chart that QT had posted.

"Ugh," she said, looking it over. "That chart is so lame! Seriously."

It felt as if I'd been carrying two wet, heavy trash bags and Sophie had come along to take one off my hands.

Later that night, I got an e-mail from Eve. From Eve! She told me she'd been reading my blog and was wondering what my last post was about. I e-mailed her back, explaining the bra-snapping problem. Then she e-mailed back, saying that used to happen in her class too, until everyone grew up a little.

CHAPTER 25

I've Grouped You in Pairs...

O ur math group is running ahead of schedule this year," Mr. Sayler announced at the beginning of one math class. "So we're going to do something a little different for the next few days." He rubbed a piece of chalk between his hands.

"The school just found this great bridge-building software," Mr. Sayler said, "and we're going to spend some time in the computer lab, working in pairs and modeling bridges. Then, when we're done, we'll build models of the bridges using toothpicks."

Hassan's hand shot up. "Do the designs have to be based on real-world bridges?"

"Well, no," Mr. Sayler said. "They'll be bridges you design yourselves. You guys can be as creative as you want, as long as the bridge is functional. And when it comes time for bridge testing, my son Ramsey's toy chest has provided the perfect vehicles." He pulled out a box of toy cars and trucks. "I've grouped you in pairs, one boy and one girl per pair."

Macy and Walker were one pair, which meant that Walker was lucky, since Macy already knew a lot about engineering.

And who was I with? Hassan, who was already clenching his jaw. I started to feel the way I did the one time I was on a sailboat—kind of seasick.

∽⚬⟩⟨⚬∿

We sat in pairs in front of the computers as Mr. Sayler showed us how we could use the software to design a bridge from start to finish—abutments to trusses, concrete to steel beams. With every choice, we'd see the cost of the bridge change. Once we'd finalized our design, we'd build and test the bridge.

Hassan and I sat at the computer. "Did he give us any limits on price?" I asked.

"I don't think so."

"Should we just get going?"

"Sure." He clicked the option to start a new design. "Abutments?" he said.

"Yeah. We have to."

"I mean, what kind of abutments? Standard? Arch?" His voice was sharp.

"Oh. Standard?"

"Okay."

"We could make it a really low bridge, really close to the water," I said.

"Okay," he said, changing the height. "But excavation raises the price a lot."

"But there are no cost limits."

"True."

It took us the whole class period to finalize the design. Getting the trusses right—lining up the supporting triangles—was hard. Our designs kept failing the stability test. It got kind of funny after a while, but Hassan wasn't laughing.

"I tried to build a sculpture out of toothpicks with my dad once," I said. "It didn't work out so well."

"They might as well be asking us to build a bridge out of feathers," Hassan said. "Toothpicks are lame."

"I think it's gonna be okay," I said.

"We'll see," he said. He turned and left the room.

I left a minute later, thinking about the Emily Dickinson poem we'd read in English. Hope was the thing with feathers. Not bridges. We'd make the toothpicks work.

That night I found this on Hassan's blog:

Tomorrow, more fun with toothpick sculptures!! Bridges, whatever! My partner seems eternally optimistic—or let's say Wishful—about the prospects.

....

QT   Arts & crafts—so much fun!!! Not. :(

The next day, a hard rain pounded against the classroom windows. Mr. Sayler handed out toothpicks and glue.

"Are there hot-glue guns?" Rebecca asked.

"Not in the budget," Mr. Sayler said.

"The glue's going to take forever to dry," Hassan said, irritated.

"You've got the rest of the year, if you need it. Study halls, lunch periods, whatever," Mr. Sayler said.

Hassan started on the abutments and roadbed, gluing toothpicks together in solid columns, while I started building the trusses. Hassan kept going to the bathroom to wash the glue off his hands. Finally, Mr. Sayler handed him a wet paper towel and said, "Just use this."

We were far behind everyone else when the class period ended. Macy and Walker's bridge looked nearly complete already, while ours was maybe 20 percent done.

We spent two more math classes on our bridge, but it still wasn't finished. "Maybe we need to work on this more in study hall," I said.

"I can't. Spelling Bee prep," Hassan said.

"Can you stay late after school tomorrow?" I asked.

He made a face. "I guess so. I'll check with my mom."

That night, he e-mailed me: "I can stay till five o'clock tomorrow."

"Okay," I wrote back. "Me too."

I e-mailed Sarah to say I wouldn't be coming home in carpool.

I hoped it would go fast. How much more one-on-one time could Hassan and I handle?

⁓◯◯⁓

Mr. Sayler left around three thirty on Friday, after all the carpools had been called over the loudspeaker. "Are you guys going to be okay?" he asked Hassan and me.

We nodded.

Our bridge's separate parts were dry and done. The trick was going to be to get the whole bridge—abutments, trusses, and roadbed—to stick together. Hassan did the gluing as I held the parts together.

After a few minutes, Hassan had an idea: he ran over to Mr. Sayler's desk, unplugged the small fan that sat by his computer, then plugged it in by us. He pointed it toward the bridge. "This will make it dry faster."

"At least it's dry outside today," I said.

"I wish we had clamps," he added. "We need clamps."

He held the abutments to the roadbed while I held the trusses to the abutments. Our hands were so tangled, bridge making was starting to feel like a game of Twister. On a distant field, middle school girls cheered on their team. Their voices sounded tinny and hollow.

Mr. Graham stopped in the classroom doorway.

"Now that's cooperative learning," he said. "I wish I had a camera."

"We could probably take turns holding the bridge," I said.

"I don't know," Hassan said.

"Just truss me," I joked. He actually cracked up (he had big white teeth), then took his hands off the bridge. I tried holding the abutments to the roadbed to the trusses all at once. It worked.

"Awesome," he said, sighing. He reached into his bag and pulled out an iPod Touch. "Jay-Z?" he asked.

"Sure."

We sat and listened to the music for a few minutes. When a Black Eyed Peas song started, we switched, and he held on to the bridge.

"I'm sorry," he said, out of the blue.

"For what?" I asked.

"For . . . not thinking the bridge would work at first."

"No problem," I said. My heart was beating fast. For a second, I'd thought he was going to tell me about his blog.

At five o'clock, our bridge wasn't 100 percent dry, but it was stable. We grabbed our backpacks and waited out in front of the school. Hassan's father glided up in a black BMW, and Hassan got in. His dad gave me a thumbs-up, and they drove off.

ᴔ) (ᴔ

I checked Hassan's blog over the weekend for more bridge commentary, but the blog was quiet.

On Monday morning, our bridge was still intact. The glue was bone-dry, and the roadbed seemed strong. In math class we stress-tested all the models. After our bridge survived the heaviest of Ramsey's toy trucks, Hassan gave me a high five. Ours wasn't the best, but it wasn't the worst either, and it seemed as if we were both completely okay with that.

ᴔ) (ᴔ

That night, I checked Hassan's blog again. The heading at the top of the screen had changed. Now it read, "QT, yo!" Underneath was a new posting.

> Everybody, wimpy Hassan doesn't want to do
> this blog anymore, so I'm taking over. QT, yo!

The timing couldn't be a coincidence, could it? I wrote a new blog post.

Bridges

As everybody probably knows by now, this week our math class did a bridge project. You might want to download the software at home or try it in the computer lab. It's free, and it's pretty cool. Hassan and I had a little trouble with our toothpick bridge at first, but in the end, we made our bridge work.

Wish #19: That all of you try this software. It's fun, and you'll never take a bridge for granted again!

CHAPTER 26

Azalea Days

Hassan's blog continued with QT in charge, though it wasn't as active as it had been. I still wondered whether I'd ever find out who QT was.

But spring had arrived in Baltimore, bursting out in leaves and flowers. I liked azaleas best of all, especially the purple ones, which looked as pretty on the ground, all bruised and soft, as they had on the bush.

My family used to take a picture of my grandfather and me in front of one of the azalea bushes in our yard every year. The tradition started because we both had birthdays around the same time—Granddad's on April 24 and mine on May 1. In the first three azalea photos, Granddad was holding me, but by the time I was four, I was standing next to him. In all the photos, he looks very proud. It was so weird not taking that picture last year. He had died the month before. Dad had suggested taking one of Ian and me, but we hadn't done it. It wouldn't have been the same.

May 1 fell on a Saturday this year, so Gran and I decided to bring birthday cupcakes to school the day before. I chose to wear my favorite pink-and-purple-striped skirt, with my favorite white  shirt, a dark purple sash, and lavender flats.

All laid out on the bed, my outfit looked like something out of *Tween Life*, something from a "great outfits under $100" page.

It was a fun day at school. We watched a movie in science class and wrote poems about pets in English. When we walked into the cafeteria for lunch, we smelled something. French fries?

"You did it, Genie!" Rebecca said, hugging me. "You're my hero! I'm getting you some new hamster erasers after school today!"

I hugged her back. A few other people gave me high fives. Had persuasive wishing worked? And was it just a coincidence that they finally brought back Junk Food Lunch on the same day I was celebrating my birthday?

The surprise was the best part of all. It felt like a party instead of just a lunch period.

After we finished our pizza and burgers and french fries, I passed out Gran's cupcakes (yellow with chocolate icing). Everyone sang "Happy Birthday." No candles were allowed—school fire policy. This was good, because it meant no official wishes for the day, and no one asking me what I had wished for. (Everyone knew you weren't supposed to tell other people your birthday-cake wishes. If you did, they wouldn't come true.)

"I swear, your grandmother makes the best cupcakes," Rebecca said, licking frosting off her fingertips, crumbs falling from her mouth. I wasn't really sure that Rebecca had ever met a cupcake she didn't like, but I said thanks anyway. Blair and Sarah took cupcakes but didn't eat them. They just picked at the icing.

There were seven cupcakes left after all the fifth graders had gotten one, so Mr. Sayler said I could walk around handing out the others with a friend. This was an HCD tradition. You always delivered extra birthday snacks to your favorite teachers from past years, and you always chose a friend to deliver them with. For the first time ever, I picked someone other than Sarah: Sophie.

When Sophie and I had finished walking the halls, I came back to Mr. Sayler's room and sat down at my desk. I looked up at the blackboard and saw a poster propped on the chalk tray.

Every time there was a birthday in the class, someone made a huge birthday poster and we all signed it. Anna Miles usually did the big letters on the poster because her lettering was the best.

It's not like the card was a surprise, but it was still pretty awesome to get it. I liked how Anna Miles wrote "Genie Wishes" instead of just "Genie." Blair wrote the shortest comment possible: "HBD2U, Blair."

In study hall Mr. Sayler let me use his computer.

Birthday

You guys are the best. I love my card!

P.S. Parents, faculty, and cafeteria staff, especially Chef Jacobs: Thanks for bringing back Junk Food Lunch!

Wish #20: That Junk Food Lunch will keep happening—every once in a while, at least!

Genie W.

CHAPTER 27

Eleven Candles

J woke up at six thirty on May 1—officially eleven years old, since I'd been born at 2:34 AM.

As a father-daughter activity for my birthday, Dad had signed us up for an Egyptian art workshop at the Walters Art Museum, one of Dad's favorite places to take Ian and me. Dad thought it would be fun, since I'd loved studying Egypt in history. We left the house at nine thirty and drove downtown.

The museum was big and clean. Even the bathrooms were elegant, with white doorways that stood tall and narrow. Uncle Mike had told me once that places you'd been to as a kid never seemed as big when you saw them as an adult, but I was sure that even when I was eighty-five years old, this place would still seem enormous.

The workshop was held on the ground floor in a special family art room furnished with tables and chairs built to fit young kids. The chairs were so short, they made Dad look like a giraffe perched on a toadstool. Every few minutes, he shifted his weight.

The teacher spoke for a while, and then we all went upstairs to look at some real Egyptian art. I had been to this part of the museum lots of times before. The canopic jars, used to store four organs that were taken out of bodies during mummification (the liver, the  lungs, the intestines, and the stomach), always freaked me out more than the mummies.

By the end of the three-hour workshop, we had an armful of creations to take home. We had made Egyptian jewelry, created mummies out of clay, and written messages in hieroglyphs.

On the way home, Dad stopped at a funky coffee place full of wobbly, mismatched chairs. We sat on a love seat upholstered in an orange, khaki, and brown plaid. A dog could throw up on it and no one would know.

I told Dad that Sarah and Blair were doing another Pip party today—the sixth they'd done together.

"Do you wish you were with them? Or with Sarah at least?"

"Not really," I said. "It's just not my thing."

At three o'clock on May 1, we had our last softball game of the season. Unfortunately, we lost. In the end, it was a 3-8 season: 3 wins, 8 losses. Not what you'd call a triumph, but still fun. Sophie's dad had baked cookies for everyone, and he gave us all participation medals that said "Girls' Softball—Come to Bat!" He shook Dad's hand and thanked him for the coaching help.

Sophie rode home from the game with Dad and me. When we got to the house, Margo was working in our backyard. She'd been doing this a lot recently, since neither Dad nor Gran really liked gardening. She gave me a big birthday hug, then went back to her weeding. She wanted the garden to look nice for the party tonight, she said.

Granddad had filled the rock garden, which was on a slope of ground right outside our back door, with crocuses, daffodils, and tulips—flowers you see all around Baltimore in the spring. But he had also put in lots of other interesting plants called succulents, which come from desert areas. They peeked around the corners of the rocks and made the ground look magical. I loved all of them, but my favorites were the hens and chicks. I liked watching every year as the hens sprouted new chicks.

chick

chick

hen

Lulu was hovering beside the door, wagging her tail and doing "down dog" poses, so Sophie and I walked her around the block. Then we lay on my bed and read old issues of *Tween Life.*

I asked Sophie if she wanted to stay for my family

birthday dinner. I said that it probably would be kind of boring and that my Uncle Mike might talk a lot about his latest inventions. But she said she'd love to. She called her mom, who said she could pick Sophie up later. It was a plan!

By seven o'clock Gran and Dad had laid out fried chicken, coleslaw, and biscuits on a table outside. We all grabbed plates and helped ourselves. Everyone— Gran, Dad, Ian, Uncle Mike, Margo, Sophie, and I—sat around in the backyard.

"How's it feel to be eleven?" Uncle Mike asked.

"Pretty good," I responded, wiping my fingers on a napkin. "The same."

"Still a tween but soon a teen," he added.

"Yep."

"Got a boyfriend yet?"

"Mike," Dad said. "She's eleven. Let's not rush things."

"Boys are intimidated by Genie because she's so

smart. That happened to my mother," Sophie said.

"That could be," Gran said. "Anyway, Genie, never hide your smarts, not for any man." Hearing Gran refer to a "man" and me in the same thought made me feel weird, as if I had just turned twenty instead of eleven.

On the kitchen counter was the strawberry short-cake Gran made from scratch every year on May 1. She always used tiny slivers of strawberry to form the words "HAPPY BIRTHDAY!" on top. We always ate it with vanilla ice cream. It was always delicious, just as good as her sand tarts, but it tasted like birthday instead of Christmas.

Dad brought out the cake with eleven candles, and everyone sang. When I blew out the candles, I secretly wished that I wouldn't have to wait until I was twelve to get my ears pierced.

Uncle Mike gave me a check for my birthday, of course. He said he didn't know what else to get me until the first No-Foul Towels came off the assembly line, but I knew he was joking. Dad and Gran gave me a laptop. I could hardly believe it, but they said I was getting older and would need it for middle school. Ian gave me an iTunes card for twenty dollars. So did Margo, which was great, because now I could buy lots of music for my new computer. Sophie said she was going to get me a copy of her new favorite book, *When You Reach Me.*

After the last slice of cake had been devoured, Gran went to bed and Uncle Mike went home. Dad and Margo stayed downstairs to clean up. Ian and Sophie and I went up to my room to get my computer—*my computer!*—set up. After that, Sophie and I sat on my bed and played Uno.

Sophie seemed extra quiet, like she had something on her mind.

"Is something wrong?" I asked.

"No," she said.

"Are you sure?"

"It's just . . . Something happened yesterday that I want to tell you, but I don't want to risk ruining your birthday."

"What is it? Just tell me."

"Okay," Sophie said, lowering her voice to a whisper. "Blair was standing next to me in carpool yesterday when a diary or something fell out of her purse. 'On the QT' was written in puffy silver ink on the cover. She picked it up quickly and stuffed it back inside."

"QT?"

"QT," she said. "Doesn't 'on the QT' mean 'quiet' or 'secret' or something?"

"Yeah," I said. "My grandmother says it sometimes."

We went to my new computer and brought up the page for "QT, yo!" We read everything through again, imagining Blair making QT's comments. Everything made sense, even the date QT had started commenting—about the same time I'd refused to write about the Pip makeup on my blog.

I thought my heart might pound out of my throat. I knew Blair and I weren't truly friends, but this?

"We have to talk to her," Sophie said.

I thought for a minute. "Let me do it. I want to wait for the right time."

"Okay," she said. "I won't say anything." And I knew she wouldn't.

When I went to sleep that night, I was thinking about Blair and Sarah, of course, but also about Sophie. What a good friend she was turning out to be. Not loud or obnoxious or loaded down with presents for me. Just there, in the best possible way.

CHAPTER 28

Aquarium Costume

The weekend after my birthday, when I was still figuring out the right time to confront Blair, Gran and I started working on my costume for the graduation party at Sarah's. I wanted to be a starfish, but she wasn't sure how we'd get the arms to stick out. She suggested that I go as an aquarium. I could wear a box that we had decorated. That way, I could include a bunch of different fish and other sea creatures. She showed me a photo online of what she was thinking of. A mother had made an aquarium costume for her son and posted a description of how she made it. I thought it was a cool idea.

Gran and I went to the craft store to get costume supplies. Since it was Saturday, the place was packed, but we found everything we needed pretty quickly. In the checkout line we ran into Sophie and her mom. They were getting stuff for her costume too! Sophie's mom, Mrs. Rodriguez, said that I should come over to their house sometime for a get-together (I was happy she didn't say "playdate"). She and Gran decided that next Friday after school would be good.

Gran and I came home and set ourselves up at the kitchen table to work on the costume. In the basement she found a box that was the perfect size. We cut out holes for my arms, body, and head, then cut one huge hole for the front of the aquarium. We papered over the outside of the box with black construction paper and the inside with aluminum foil. Then we glued a piece of clear vinyl inside the front wall of the aquarium to look like glass. I started cutting fish and shark shapes out of construction paper, then glued them to the inside of the vinyl. A few minutes later, I found an old toy that looked like a big three-dimensional asterisk and glued that to the bottom of the aquarium. That would be a sea urchin.

I tried the finished box on with what I'd be wearing at the real party: a light blue long-sleeved leotard top and a skirt that was light blue and dark green. It was the same skirt I had worn when I'd taken my birthday cupcakes to school, but in a different color. I ran into Dad's room to show the costume to him and danced around. He thought it was awesome.

After dinner, Gran got a phone call. It was Eve's grandmother! She and Eve had come to town for the weekend and were wondering if Gran and I might be free to meet at Hooper's Books for coffee in an hour.

I was going to meet Eve!

Gran and I changed clothes, drove to the bookstore, and parked. We threaded our way toward the back of the store, where the café was. Gran pointed to a far table, where a gray-haired woman and a teenage girl sat together. The girl had thick black glasses. The ends of her dark hair were dyed a peacock blue.

She stood up and shook my hand: "Hi, I'm Eve."

"Hi!" I said. She was taller than me, but not by a lot.

We all got drinks—Eve got a chai, so I tried one too—and slices of chocolate cake, and Gran chatted with Eve's grandmother while I talked to Eve. I thought I knew her well from reading the blog, but meeting her in person was a new thing. I'd never heard her kind of croaky voice or seen her dramatic hand gestures.

We talked about everything—the bra snapping, the competing blogs, and fifth grade generally. "Right," she said. "Fifth grade. That's when everything started to get weird."

"What do you mean?"

"Oh, you know—all that stupid popularity stuff. That's the year it hit our class."

She was right. I hadn't really thought of it that way before. At the beginning of the year, we had felt

like one class—one big, uncut cake. Now we were slicing off into different groups.

"Do you like blogging?" she asked, flipping the
blue tips of her hair back over her shoulders.

"Yeah," I said. It occurred to me that I really did
like blogging, especially when people listened and
responded.

"Will you continue when the year is over?"

"Do you think I should?" I asked.

"Definitely," she said. "You're good. I should put
you on my list of guest bloggers. Some weeks, I'm
burned out."

I was smiling so broadly, I thought my face might
break.

On Friday, Sophie's mom picked us up from school.
Her car had only two doors, so you had to push down
the front seat to climb into the back. Also, it was a
stick shift, so every once in a while, the car jerked and
paused. My dad's Honda was even older than I was,

but it had four doors and no stick shift, and Gran's Toyota wasn't a stick shift either.

To get to Sophie's house, we went past my neighborhood, then kept driving to an area of Baltimore I'd never seen. I saw a big body of water surrounded by a low wall. "That's Lake Montebello," Mrs. Rodriguez said. "It's a reservoir."

Sophie's house was about the same size as our house, but the basement was a real room, with a big table, a sofa, a television, and lots of toys scattered around.

Sophie was going to the graduation party as a sea horse. Her mom had sewn the basic costume structure already, but we had to decorate it.

Sophie started rummaging around in some plastic bags. "Okay, we've got sequins and sparkly glue and ribbons. Then when that's done, Mom will hook up the strings that will tie the sea horse onto the front of me."

"What are you going to wear with it?"

"Probably just a T-shirt and some shorts. Mom thinks it'll be warm that night."

I thought about my plan to wear a long-sleeved leotard and wondered whether I should wear a sleeveless shirt instead. Sophie's mom was right. It probably *would* be warm.

While we worked on her costume, Sophie told me that her parents had adopted both her and her younger brother, Wyatt, as babies from the same orphanage in Colombia. So even though they weren't technically siblings, they had shared roots. I was really surprised to hear that Sophie and Wyatt were adopted. To me, the whole family looked so much alike, like a family you'd see in a photo frame at a store.

"Did you talk to Blair yet?" Sophie asked.

"I keep wanting to, but it's never the right time," I said. "If it doesn't happen in the next week, I'm just going to call her on the phone."

"I look at the QT blog every few days," Sophie said.

"Me too," I said.

"It's pretty boring. Mostly links to YouTube videos."

"Yeah," I said.

"Have you heard of any bra snapping recently?"

"Not really. And that chart on the blog hasn't changed for a while."

"What would Sarah think if she found out that Blair was QT?" Sophie said.

"I think she'd be mad," I said. It was hard to be sure.

"I mean, Blair did a lot of the bra snapping herself!"

"I know."

"Are you gonna tell Sarah after you talk to Blair?"

"Maybe," I said. "I haven't decided."

Mrs. Rodriguez came downstairs with cheese puffs and lemonade. "We'd better take a break so we don't mess up the costume," Sophie said.

Wyatt, Sophie's little brother, ran across the basement rug wearing nothing but a bathing suit and water wings.

I started laughing. So did Sophie.

"He's practicing for summer," Sophie said. "We just joined Fallsway Pool."

"That's where we go!" I said.

"Cool!" she said. "Is it fun there?"

"Definitely," I said.

I'd always wished I had a school friend at Fallsway. Sarah and a lot of other classmates belonged to fancier clubs, the kind built around old mansions. I had my pool friends, but having Sophie there too would make being at Fallsway even more fun.

The air in the room felt lighter now, as if Wyatt and his water wings had chased out a dark cloud.

CHAPTER 29

Sky-Blue Snowballs

J n the middle of May, Dad decided we should take Ian out to dinner to celebrate his being so responsible about his part-time job. Ian got off work at seven o'clock, so one night at 6:55 Dad and I parked near Let Freedom Ring. When we came around the corner from the parking lot, Ian was in the eagle costume, jumping on and off the curb in a steady rhythm, swiveling his hips right and left. His eagle beak was bobbing up and down as he listened to his MP3 player. He'd come a long way since I saw him at work that first time, doing the just-barely-a-wave wave.

Dad tapped Ian on the shoulder. Ian startled slightly, feathers fluttering. He pulled off the eagle head, took out his earbuds, and cleared his throat. "Hey."

"Hey," Dad said. "How'd you like to go out to dinner? Margo's gonna meet us around the corner at the Mexican place." That was Ian's favorite restaurant.

"Margo?" he said, groaning.

"She *is* my girlfriend, Ian."

At dinner, Margo asked Ian and me what we were doing for the summer. I said that I didn't have a job or anything but was doing some half-day camps and had just found out that my friend Sophie would be going to our pool.

Ian said he wasn't sure about his summer plans. He acted like Margo's question had come out of the blue, which was stupid. It was a perfectly normal grown-up-type question, but he made his voice hard and flat when he answered.

Summer Is Almost Here!

Believe it or not, the school year is finally coming to a close. Soon lower school will be just a place we used to go.

My dad likes this café called Reboot. It's a pretty cool name. I'm thinking of this summer as a kind of rebooting. There's lower school, and there's middle school. Between them, we recharge and reboot. So, what are you guys doing this summer?

Wish #21: That summer is awesome.

....

DREW   Rock band camp! Rrrrrrah!

....

SOPHIE   Fallsway Pool! :)

....

MACY   Going to the beach. Working for my dad. And rereading the *Lord of the Rings* trilogy.

....

BLAIR   Camp with Sare Bear!!!!!!

....

SARAH   Yay!!!!!!!!!!!

....

WALKER   Resuming my brave and unending quest for the city's best sky-blue snowball.

~∞)) ((∞~

Around nine o'clock that night, I knocked on Ian's
door. I was still thinking about the Blair/QT thing, but
I didn't want to tell Dad or Gran, because they'd automatically tell the school, and I wasn't ready for that.

"What?" Ian said.

"Hey," I said, opening the door. "Can I ask you
something?"

"As long as it's not related to Dad's new girlfriend,
clothes, or Dad's new girlfriend's clothes."

"It's not."

I told him about my blogging, the other blog, and
the bridge building. I told him about Hassan and QT
and Blair. I asked him what to do.

"Blair. Do I know Blair?"

"She's the one who's new this year."

"The one who's tight with Sarah?"

"That one."

Ian said that I shouldn't tell Mr. Sayler. I had Blair
in a perfect spot. She wouldn't want Sarah to know

what she'd been doing. All I had to do was confront her about it and she'd fold like a piece of origami. "QT, yo!" would be no more.

Why hadn't I talked to him about all of this before? It all seemed so clear when he looked at it!

I thanked him and left the room as soon as I could. He might have been willing to consult on this problem, but that still didn't mean I should linger in the doorway, chatting for the rest of the night.

∽◐) (◑∾

In English the next day, Walker asked me if I'd ever had a sky-blue snowball. I said I hadn't.

"Why not?" he asked.

"What do they taste like?"

"Blue."

"Blue?"

"Blue. Electric blue. Like lightning."

He told me that the best sky-blue snowballs he'd found so far were sold right behind the entrance to Portham, a university north of Baltimore. My family and I drove by Portham sometimes, on the way to the mall. We'd be cruising along this winding avenue, and all of a sudden we'd see a little stone building—a gatehouse, I think Gran called it—with the Portham sign out front. It looked like a magical place, the kind of place where elves would go to build shoes. I'd never noticed the snowball stand.

The next day, Gran had to get to school extra early for a meeting, so I was the first person in class. Mr. Sayler said he was glad I was there so early because he wanted to ask me if I'd like to take care of his son, Ramsey, a few afternoons a week over the summer. He or his wife could bring Ramsey to my house, and then I could watch him, and Gran would be there in case we needed anything. Ramsey would take a nap for part of each afternoon. Then Mr. Sayler or his wife would pick Ramsey up. Mr. Sayler said that he had already talked to Gran about this, and she liked the idea.

I said yes right away. I definitely wanted some walking-around money for myself. I could use it to buy snowballs, for one thing.

During recess, I finally found my time alone with Blair. We were all playing kickball. Blair was in right field, and I was playing first base. Jack kicked a ball way over my head. I ran back and soon found myself in the outfield near Blair, both of us watching the tomato-red ball fly over the chain-link fence and into the dense woods behind the school. I started around the fence and into the woods, then turned back toward Blair. "Are you coming?"

She shrugged and followed me.

"Ugh," she said, kicking through some brush. "Why don't they just cut down all these trees?"

We wandered around for a minute, looking.

"Here it is," she said, picking up the ball and brushing off some leaves.

"I need to ask you something," I said.

"What? You want to order some makeup? Oh little one, you're growing up!"

"No," I said. "I want to know about QT."

"What?" she said, screwing up her face.

"Hassan's blog?"

"What blog?"

Suddenly the day was hot and my face hotter. "Nothing," I said. "Forget I mentioned it."

We started walking back toward the school—me in front, Blair carrying the ball behind me.

"Wait a minute," she said. "It's me."

I turned around and stared at her. I'd known deep down that she was QT, yet her confession still came as a shock.

"Please please please, don't tell Sare."

"Why not?"

"Just don't, Genie. *Please.*" She started to cry, silent tears falling down her face, streaking her tinted moisturizer.

"Why shouldn't I?"

"I'll take the blog down today," she sobbed.

"Today?"

"The minute I get home."

I thought about it for a second. Images flashed before my eyes. Me telling Sarah, Sarah's eyes opening wide, Blair begging forgiveness. It was tempting, briefly. I might have enjoyed putting Blair and Sarah's friendship in jeopardy, but I didn't want to hurt Sarah.

"Okay," I said. "Deal."

"Deal," Blair said, wiping her eyes with the back of her hands. "Thanks."

That night, I typed in the URL for the QT blog, but it pulled up only some random advertisement. The blog was down!

I called Sophie and told her about the confrontation in the woods.

"Oh my God!" she said. "I knew it, I knew it, I knew it!"

"I know."

"We have to tell everyone. Especially Sarah."

I explained my decision. Blair and I had made a pact, and she'd taken the blog down. Unless Blair went back on the promise, I wouldn't say anything.

After weeks of worries related to the blog, I felt peaceful, like a dog that settles down to rest after circling and circling. I had the answers I needed, but I wasn't going to use them to win Sarah back. That would have been a Blair-type move, and I wasn't Blair.

CHAPTER 30

Rehearsals

n ow that the blog drama had played itself out, there was a new performance to prepare for: lower school graduation. One hot spring day, right before lunch, Mr. Sayler handed out a sheet of graduation guidelines. We read them through as a class.

The girls were supposed to wear any kind of pastel-colored dress, and the boys were supposed to wear dark blazers with white button-down shirts, khaki pants, and a tie. Each student would be given five tickets for friends and family. I counted inside my head: Dad, Gran, Ian, and Uncle Mike. That was four. If my grandfather or mother had still been alive or if Margo hadn't had to work that morning, we'd need that fifth seat, but as it was, I couldn't think of a fifth person. I'd just have to give the extra ticket to someone with a bigger family.

"Are we going to have a valedictorian?" Hassan asked expectantly.

"Not for the lower school graduation," Mr. Sayler responded. "Instead, we have a few students who perform different functions. Does anyone know what they are?"

Rebecca raised her hand. "There's the person who passes the senior cup to a current fourth grader."

"That's one."

"Someone leads the school song," Sam said.

"That's two. Who's the third?"

Jack raised his hand. "Bobert the cheese man?"

Everyone laughed hysterically. The names Bob and Bobert and the word *cheese* could be said as the punch line to anything, and we would all laugh. We loved those words as much as we still hated *playdate* and *puberty*.

"What is a cheese man, anyway?" Mr. Sayler

asked. "A man who sells cheese, a man who likes cheese, or a man made of cheese?"

"Yes," Sarah said.

"Yes?" Mr. Sayler echoed.

"All those things," Sarah clarified.

Mr. Sayler ran a hand over his bald head and sighed. "Okay," he continued, "the third person is actually the person who sums up what the year has been like for the class and expresses the class's wishes for the next year. It's kind of like what Genie does in her blog, but condensed into a single speech, called the class speech. However, Genie won't be the one doing it. That's not to say you haven't done a terrific job, Genie, because you have. We just want to hear from someone else this time around."

Mr. Sayler announced the three students who had been chosen for the honorary positions. Hassan would be passing the senior cup to the fourth grader. Bethany would be leading the school song. And Sophie would be doing the class speech—a cool choice, I thought.

We started daily rehearsals for graduation, which would take place in the auditorium. During rehearsals, we fifth graders would sit on the stage—girls in the front rows, boys in the back rows—while the teachers would sit in the audience.

Bethany, Hassan, and Sophie would rehearse their individual parts. Bethany would practice walking to the front of the stage and saying, "Please rise to sing the school song." Then all of us would stand up. Mr. Frazier, the music teacher, would play the song on the piano, and we'd all start singing. Sometimes he'd lift a hand off the keys and raise it up, shouting "More! More!" but the sound wouldn't change much. Most fifth graders didn't want to look too excited about singing something as boring as a school song.

Later in the rehearsals, Hassan would stand up and a fourth grader, Bryce, would walk to the stage to practice receiving the senior cup. Hassan was at least a foot taller than Bryce, so Bryce had to crane his neck up as Hassan gave his speech:

We, the senior class of the Hopkins Country Day Lower School, pass this, the senior cup, to you, the new senior class. The cup is a symbol of loyalty, hard work, integrity, honesty, and good sportsmanship, all of which we strive for at HCD.

Finally, Sophie would practice her speech. She began by reminiscing about our first year at HCD and what we must have looked like on the first day of kinder-garten. Then she talked about things we'd learned each year with different teachers and about classmates who had left along the way. She finished by speculating about what we had to look forward to in middle school: new freedoms, new challenges, new friendships. The speech even mentioned my blog post about using the summer to reboot.

During rehearsals, Blair and Sarah kept turning around to talk to the boys. It reminded me of the holi-day wrap party, when Blair and Sarah were wrapping and flirting at the same time.

"Girls," Mr. Sayler kept saying to Blair and Sarah, "eyes forward, mouths shut." Until Blair came along, I'd almost never heard a teacher tell Sarah to stop doing something. Now it happened a lot.

A couple of times, Mr. Graham came into the auditorium to rehearse the handing out of diplomas. Shake with your right hand, take with your left. That was all we had to remember, but it was hard to do correctly, especially when you thought about it too much.

The rehearsals were boring, of course, but we couldn't help feeling a little excited. After all, this was *graduation* we were practicing for.

∞◯) (◯∞

After rehearsal one day, I was sitting at a huge lunch table with almost all the girls in the class. To my right were Rebecca, Sarah, and Blair.

"Guys, I have *nothing* to wear to Sarah's party yet," Rebecca said.

"I was thinking about going to one of those cheesy

costume stores and just buying whatever mermaid costume fits me," Sarah said.

"Oh my God," Blair said, "the three of us, you and me and Becs, could be mermaids together!"

"I love it," Rebecca said. "But do we get the costumes at the cheesy store?"

"We could just get them online," Sarah said. "We'll have tons more to choose from."

"And then we can figure out what makeup to wear with them!" Blair said.

"Yay!" Sarah said, clapping her hands.

To my left sat Sophie, Macy, and Anna Miles. Sophie and Macy were watching intently as Anna Miles sketched on a napkin the sea urchin costume she and her dads were making for the party. No one was squealing or clapping, but everyone was happy.

The next morning, in front of Blair's locker, the mermaids could not stop talking about the costumes

Mrs. White had ordered for them online: what the different colors of the outfits were, what they would do with their hair, what they would wear for shoes. And, of course, which Pip products would work best for sea goddesses. Some of the boys got involved in the conversation too. I didn't.

CHAPTER 37

Shipley Bowl

On graduation morning, I woke up early—like at six—and typed a blog entry.

Graduation Day!

I can't believe it's finally here—graduation day! So, happy graduation day! And happy no-more-graduation-rehearsals day!

I feel like a lot has happened this year. Jack learned he wasn't allowed to come to an all-girls slumber party, no matter how adorable his sleeping bag was. Many of us learned how to build bridges (virtual ones, at least). The girls learned that certain combinations of anatomical structures look a lot like rams' heads. But we all made it to the end of the ride.

Wish #22: That middle school proves to be even better than lower school.

⁘⁙) (⁙⁘

That morning, we gathered in our classroom the same way we did every school morning, but this time we were all dressed up. On Mr. Sayler's desk sat two boxes marked "Park View Flowers." The long, skinny box held long-stemmed yellow roses with no thorns. Each girl would carry one. The second box held the boys' boutonnieres, which were also yellow roses.

My dress was a pale lavender with light yellow trim—something that Gran and I had found on a clearance rack. And I had on my lavender flats, which Gran had cleaned to look new.

In their blazers and loafers and ties, the boys looked older, like they were middle schoolers already. Mr. Sayler and Rebecca's mother went around the room pinning boutonnieres to lapels. It was good that there were adults on hand to help: the boys who tried to do it themselves ended up with flowers pitched sideways.

Mrs. Baumann had on a really pretty gray dress with a forest-green scarf. When she wasn't pinning on boutonnieres, she was hugging us and saying she couldn't believe how grown-up we all were. A couple of the boys looked stiff when she hugged them, but everyone else hugged her back.

Sarah, Blair, and Rebecca were standing in a corner holding their flowers and passing a cherry-colored lip gloss around. Rebecca offered me some, but I said no thanks. Sarah had her elbow hooked into Blair's and was laughing, laughing, laughing. She looked as happy as I'd ever seen her.

We lined up in the hallway as Mr. Frazier played the piano. Through the door to the auditorium I spotted my family lined up on one bench. My father was tallest, followed by my uncle, my brother, and finally my grandmother.

The fifth-grade girls were in order by height. So were the boys. Sophie stood right in front of me, ready for her speech, holding note cards worn soft at the corners. She turned around and smiled weakly at me.

Immediately behind me stood Blair. "Sam looks so adorable in his husky-sized blue blazer. I wonder whether he's going to call you over the summer?"

"Leave him alone, Blair."

"Is your neighborhood crush here to see you? What was his name? Luke?"

"There is no neighborhood crush," I said. "I made him up to get you off my back. Having a crush is not a requirement for completing fifth grade!"

Blair's glossy cherry lips went still. She was silent. Silent! Blair!

Finally, Mr. Frazier started the marching-in music, and we all started singing. We proceeded down the aisle and onto the stage, where we stood in front of our seats. The lights of the stage were warmer and brighter than I had expected. I caught Gran's eye and smiled. Uncle Mike and Dad smiled at me too.

Mr. Graham came up to the lectern to welcome everyone. He said a few words about the history of HCD. Then, right on cue, Bethany stood up and crossed to the center of the stage. She gestured for everyone to rise, and we all did—graduates, faculty, family, friends. Bethany sounded calm when she said her line about the school song, but I could see her ankles trembling.

Mr. Graham returned to the stage to hand out awards. Hassan got the Hopkins Prize, which went to the student with the highest grade point average. Jack received the Baker Award, for athletics. Then I got something called the Shipley Bowl. When I heard my name, I stood up and put the yellow rose on my seat. The applause swelled in my ears and carried me forward. I shook Mr. Graham's hand (with my right) and took the silver bowl he handed me (with my left). A number of other awards followed, but I was having a hard time listening. What had my bowl been for? I hadn't even heard.

Next came Hassan's presentation of the silver cup. Finally, there was Sophie's speech. She did it exactly as rehearsed, but she sounded even livelier and more confident than she had during rehearsals. I could see her parents smiling in the audience. Wyatt sat on Mrs. Rodriguez's lap in a pair of cargo shorts, swinging his bare legs.

Mr. Graham handed out our diplomas, then ended with a few words about how much he would miss us next year, even though we'd be just in the next building.

We filed out of the auditorium, past the Shipley Clock, then walked outside for a class picture. The photographer arranged everyone by height, with the taller people in the back. That's where I was, between Blair and Sophie again. The photographer took a few photos, then sent us off to meet our families in the cafeteria for the reception. Someone had put out baskets of flowers, but it was still just the cafeteria. Mr. Sayler congratulated me on getting the Shipley Bowl and said he'd call me next week to talk more about babysitting.

Before we left school, my family and I took the Shipley Bowl, with my name now added to the others engraved on it, back to the library, where it lived. Uncle

Mike went over to the shelves of *National Geographic* magazines and started flipping through the oldest ones until he found a photo of an African woman wearing no shirt.

"Helen Kunkle, in the name of all that is right and good, what filth are you exposing these children to?" he asked.

Ian laughed and Dad shook his head.

"Oh Mike," Gran said. "You're worse than the kids."

The Shipley Bowl's case was right in the middle of the periodicals. Gran used her key to open the case door and returned the bowl to its spot. I liked the fact that my name was engraved on the bowl, even if Haddock Kunkle still sounded pretty awful, like the name of a weird musical instrument. It was nice to know that a part of me would be staying behind in the lower school even as the rest of me moved on.

"What was it for?" I asked Gran as she locked the case. "I was too surprised to pay attention."

"Well, read the bowl," she said, pointing.

"The Shipley Bowl," I read, "awarded to a student who displays mastery of the written word."

"See?" she said.

"Wow," I said. "That's nice."

Mr. Graham was walking through the front lobby as we were leaving. "Congratulations on the Shipley Bowl, Genie," he said, shaking my hand. It was the third time I'd shaken his hand that day.

"Thanks," I said.

"I was a big fan of your blog," he added.

Gran smiled. "We're very proud of Genie."

"Keep up the good work," he said to me. "And have a great summer!"

The Indian restaurant wasn't far from school, so we all walked over, Gran and Uncle Mike leading the pack, followed by Dad and me, trailed by Ian. We walked past Tudor-style row houses with neat, colorful gardens. The air was warm but not yet humid.

When we got to the restaurant, housed on the first floor of what my grandmother called "a grand old apartment building," Margo was already sitting at a round table near the window. She was wearing a bright red dress. She squeezed my shoulders and kissed my cheek. Before we went to the buffet, we passed around my diploma. It was small, about the size of an envelope.

Gran told her about the Shipley Bowl, and Margo hugged me again. "That's amazing, Genie! Maybe you'll follow me into journalism someday."

"Maybe," I said.

The waiter brought a basket of peppery cracker-type things and an assortment of dipping sauces. I didn't know what any of it was, but it tasted great.

"Ian, before I forget," Margo said, "my brother Tom told me you've been a terrific employee."

"Thanks," Ian said. "Tom's cool." For the first time, he seemed to soften toward Margo. He actually looked her in the eye, which I'd never seen him do before.

"I'm glad you like him," Margo said.

Then Margo handed me a square velvet box. Inside

was a pair of tiny pierced silver hoops just like I'd always wanted. I looked at the earrings, then at her, then at Dad. Dad shrugged his shoulders.

She winked at me, then whispered behind her hand, so only I could see: "I'm working on him."

I walked quickly into the bathroom and held the earrings up to my ears. Then I pinched my earlobes with my fingernails to see what piercing them would feel like. It wasn't *so* bad.

"Dad," I said when I got back to the table, "can I really get my ears pierced soon?"

"Maybe," he said.

"This summer?"

"Maybe."

"Before school starts?"

"I'll think about it."

"Definitely?"

"Is it hot in here, or is it just me?" Dad asked, fanning himself with the wine list.

CHAPTER 32

Night Swimming

J couldn't figure out how to sit in the car in my aquarium costume. I didn't want to squash the box. "I could just lean forward in the seat," I said to Dad. "That'll work."

"Just take it off until we get there," he said.

"But then someone might see me before I have it on."

"So?"

We both laughed. He was right.

It was a warm night, so I had chosen a sleeveless shirt instead of the long-sleeved leotard I was wearing when I first tried the costume on. I still thought it was a really cool costume, and I couldn't wait to see Sophie as the sea horse.

"So, do you feel like it was a good year overall?" Dad asked.

"Yeah," I said.

"I'm incredibly proud of you for getting that bowl. I mean, I'm proud of you for a million reasons, but that was the million and first."

"Thanks."

We were stopped at what Dad always claimed was the longest red light in the whole city. The light usually made Dad impatient, but not tonight.

"Blogs seem kind of silly sometimes," he said, "but I liked yours. You did a good job of talking about things that matter to your class, and I could tell that everyone really respected you for it."

"How?"

"I don't know. It was just the sense I got, seeing the other kids with you today. Are you going to run for class blogger next year?"

"Probably not," I said. "I actually really liked blogging, but because I was doing it for the whole class, I sometimes felt like I couldn't say exactly what I wanted to. Maybe I'll start my own blog, like Eve did."

"That'd be great."

"Eve might ask me to guest blog on her site. Wouldn't that be cool?"

"Absolutely."

"Maybe Sophie could run for class blogger next year. She'd be good at it."

"Sophie's a neat girl. I've enjoyed getting to know her."

"Me too."

"Friendships change over time, which sometimes means letting old friends go," he said. "But you already know that, don't you?"

"I guess so."

"It's all part of growing up—which you, my dear, are doing beautifully."

Dad hugged me for an extra long time. "You packed all your regular swim stuff in your bag?" he asked.

"Yep."

"A towel too?"

"Yep."

"And you'll call if you want to leave before ten thirty?"

"Yep."

Dad was so adorably Dad-like sometimes.

We parked in front of Sarah's house, and Dad walked around to my side of the car to help me slip the aquarium box on. He kissed me and told me to have fun.

One arm hanging stiffly on either side of the box, I walked up the marble staircase to the door, feeling more nervous than I had for graduation itself.

Mrs. White answered the door in a mermaid costume. She looked me up and down: "Hi, Genie—wow! What a neat costume! Your family is always so *creative!*"

"Thanks, Mrs. White."

"And congratulations on winning the Shipley Bowl. Don't tell him I told you, but Mr. White won the same award when he was at HCD a million years ago." As she said this, Mr. White walked up, shaking his head and smiling.

"Well, go on back!" Mrs. White said. "Nora's out at a friend's tonight, thank goodness!"

⁓⊙) (⊙⤳

Rebecca, Blair, and Sarah were standing over by some tiki torches. They all had their hair in ponytails and were wearing the same shimmery pink lipstick.

"Oh my God, Genie, I love your costume!" Sarah said, touching the box.

"So this is the aquarium, huh? You and your grandmother *made* this? It's awesome," Rebecca added. "I love love love it."

Blair just looked at me.

Drew ran over, dragging Jack. They were both dressed as pirates. "Sarah, just so you know, Jack is saying all kinds of stuff behind your back." Drew was laughing as Jack punched him in the side. They raced away.

"What?" Sarah shouted, running off after them, with Rebecca and Blair in pursuit.

I looked around the backyard. Macy the clown fish,

Anna Miles the purple sea urchin, and Sophie the sea horse were talking over by the food. A few of the guys, like Walker, were dressed as blue crabs, and someone else was a lobster. The fence around the pool area was hung with posters of sea creatures: a whale, a dolphin, an octopus—even a manatee.

While I was thinking about how much I love manatees, Hassan—dressed as Neptune—walked up to me. He was wearing a grass skirt and Mardi Gras beads and carrying a trident. Out of the blue, he apologized for starting his blog, which he said was a stupid idea right from the start.

I wasn't sure how to respond, except to thank him for the apology. Apologies from the gods were hard to come by.

I hung out with Sophie, Macy, and Anna Miles for a while. Then everyone went to go change into their swim clothes—everyone except Anna Miles and

Macy, who said they didn't feel like swimming. Macy whispered to me that she'd gotten her period for the first time the day before.

"Oh my God!" I said.

"It's not a big deal," Macy said. "I just don't feel like swimming."

The boys went into Nora's room, and the girls went into Sarah's room. I had brought my two-piece from the Rapids. I put it on, wrapped a towel around my waist, rested my aquarium box and regular clothes in a corner of the room, and ran back outside.

We all stood around the edge of the pool. The sky was dark now, but the backyard was lit by the torches and some lights from the house. We got instructions from the lifeguards the Whites had hired. No pushing, no dunking, no running, no rough play. And have fun.

We played Sharks and Minnows for a long time, then switched to Marco Polo. I wasn't used to playing in the pool with so many people. It wasn't a big pool, so we were constantly bumping into the boys. In the classroom, we had at least a desk's worth of space between us and were wearing more clothes. This night swimming was more awkward. Drew was still paying a lot of attention to Blair, Hassan and Rebecca were talking in a corner of the pool, and Jack was tickling Sarah all the time.

I slipped under the water to smooth out my hair, and when I came back up, Sam was standing over me. "Eek," I said. "You scared me." Was he looking down the top of my bathing suit?

"You were a really good blogger," he said. "That's why I told you about Hassan's blog."

In all my wondering about who QT was, I'd forgotten to figure out who'd told me about Hassan's blog in the first place. Sam. First, he was my Secret Friend, and then he was my friend who told me a secret.

"Thanks," I said.

"Why didn't you tell the other girls?" he asked.

"I was just glad when that blog was gone," I said.

I climbed out of the pool in the shallow end, where the stairs were. Macy and Anna Miles were still dry, sitting in some chairs, next to a dripping-wet Sophie.

I grabbed my towel, wrapped it back around my waist, and sat down with them.

"What are you doing this summer?" Macy asked me.

"I'm doing a few half-day camps at MAC. And I'm going to take care of Mr. Sayler's son, Ramsey, a few afternoons a week."

"How cool is that?" Anna Miles said. "I would love that!"

"And we're both gonna be at Fallsway a lot," Sophie said. "I want to learn to do a cartwheel off the diving board."

"Me too!" I said.

The parents started gathering in the backyard around ten fifteen. When Dad and Margo came, I collected my stuff from upstairs and hugged my friends good-bye. Sophie told me to call her in the morning. Maybe we could meet at the pool, she said.

On the drive home, we stopped in an area of Baltimore I'd never seen before, so Margo could drop a book off for a friend of hers. While she was inside the friend's house, Dad and I walked around a huge brick office building that had once been a factory. Some rusted metal wheels, or cogs—I wasn't sure what they were called—were welded into a railing on one side of the building. I imagined them spinning slowly alongside each other, along their interlocking teeth: making things happen, making things work.

It would take me a few weeks to slip into summer mode. There were a lot of things to look forward to. Neighborhood walks with Lulu. Afternoons with Ramsey. Walking-around money. Pool stuff with Sophie. Bedtime in my air-conditioned room, getting lost in a new book. Maybe even getting my ears pierced!

Hello, Middle Schoolers!

It's weird swimming at night, isn't it? I love how the water gets lit by the moonlight, and there's no bright sun to make you squint.

As Sophie said in her class speech, today we are saying good-bye to our lower-school selves and starting to form our middle-school selves. We're like sea creatures trading up for bigger shells. The shell will change, but we'll still be the same creatures on the inside.

Thanks for electing me to be your class blogger—spokesperson for your wishes, hopes, and dreams. I'll grant you three wishes. I can't promise anything, but I hope they'll all come true.

Have a great summer. See you in September.

Love, Genie

ABOUT THE AUTHOR

Elisabeth Dahl writes for children and adults from her home in Baltimore, Maryland, where she lives with her family. This is her first book. Visit her online at elisabethdahl.com.

This book was designed by Sara Corbett and art directed by Chad W. Beckerman. The text in this book is set in Odile, a typeface designed by Sibylle Hagmann in 2006. Odile is a reinterpretation of Charter, a typeface William Addison Dwiggins began designing in the 1930s but never finished. Other typefaces in this book include Auto, Elroy, and Prater.

The cover illustration is by Karl Kwasny.

This book was printed and bound by R. R. Donnelley in Crawfordsville, Indiana. Its production was overseen by Alison Gervais.